CARNIVAL GIRL

CARNIVAL GIRL

MAX GARETH

CUTTING EDGE

ISBN-13: 978-1-952138-80-5

Published by
Cutting Edge Books
PO Box 8212
Calabasas, CA 91372
www.cuttingedgebooks.com

CHAPTER ONE

I t was a spring rain; a steady, ground-soaking downpour that was going to go on all night.

Inside the diner, Norma sat in a booth at one end and stared at her reflection in the window. The rain pelted the glass, distorting the image, and Norma looked at her face with fascination. She had the impression of seeing herself underwater. It was like watching herself drown.

A cash register clanged. Norma took her eyes from the window and looked down the length of the narrow counter. The hip-spread, blowzy waitress was making change for a truck driver who was probing his teeth and casting short glances along the diner to where Norma was sitting. Lowering her eyes, Norma stared into the thick white cup that was half-filled with cold coffee.

"Nice night for a drive," the waitress said.

"If ya got a paddle," the man answered.

"Yeah." The girl snickered and patted one hip. "Well, don't take no wooden nickles." She turned away and went to the end of the counter to lean her heavy breasts in front of three men who sat talking in low tones.

The truck driver pulled his collar up and zipped his jacket to his neck. He took one last look at Norma, then slid back the door of the diner, and stepped into the rain, slamming the door.

Norma lifted her eyes from the cup. She took a deep breath and sighed. She lifted a hand to rub her tired eyes, then she ran the hand lightly over her thick, black hair. It was still wet. I must look like a drowned cat, she thought. Her raincoat, hanging at the end of the booth was still dripping. The cotton dress she was wearing was also wet. It clung to the full, rounded curves of her body, emphasizing the fact that she wore nothing under the dress. She could feel the eyes from the end of the counter on her. She knew what the three men were looking at, and was too tired to care. Her eyes were closed, and she leaned back against the booth.

"Anything else, hon?"

Norma opened her eyes and looked up at the waitress. The woman was open-faced, smiling. Her expression was warm, but curious.

"You oughta get something good and hot inside you," the waitress said. "Wet like that, you'll catch your death of cold." She cocked her head and waited expectantly.

"I guess you're right," Norma said. Her voice had a deep, a warm, liquid sound. Her finger came up and touched the dime that was next to the coffee cup. She pushed it towards the waitress. "But that's all the money I have," she said.

The waitress pursed her lips, then her wide mouth broke away from her teeth. "Hell, hon," she said, "I guess this old joint could stand one on the house." She turned and padded away on her foot-shaped crepe soles.

Watching the woman's back, Norma felt something tug at her and she bit down on her lower lips and swallowed. After her last experience, she expected kindness from no one, but the woman's obvious compassion affected her.

The waitress brought back the cup of hot coffee and put it down. "This will perk you up," she said.

Norma smiled. "Thank you," she said softly.

"Hungry?"

Norma shook her head.

"You wouldn't kid an old hand, would you? Hell, hon, I been down myself. Believe me, you can run farther and faster with something under the belt."

"I had a big lunch," Norma said. That was true. The man in the big Buick who had picked her up in the morning, had been more than gracious. He was interested in her welfare and he insisted that she eat anything that she wanted for lunch. Later on, as the afternoon wore into dusk, he had brought the bottle of whiskey from the glove compartment. They had been driving through the heavy rain for an hour and he had pulled over to the side for a drink. When Norma said that she didn't drink, his interest in her welfare began to wan. When he couldn't get her in the back seat he was gracious enough to open the car door and put her out into the rain. She had enough wrong-side-of-the-tracks know-how in her to curse the disappearing tail-lights, as she set out to walk the half-mile to the diner.

"I'll make you a ham sandwich," the waitress proposed. "Maybe you'll be hungry when you see it." She went away again.

Norma sugared the coffee and then stirred it, staring absently into the bowels of the long, narrow diner, grateful for the warm-lighted shelter. But she couldn't stay there forever and she had to think ahead. What was she going to do? The thought of going back into the bone-chilling rain was depressing.

"Here y'are, hon." The waitress placed the sandwich on the table.

"You're awful kind," Norma said.

"Just making up for all the bad things I already done," the waitress grinned pertly.

Seeing the sandwich did make Norma hungry. She lifted it and took a bite.

"See, I told ya. Nothing like the sight of food to get the stomach aching for it. Mind if I sit down." The waitress didn't wait for an answer, but slid into the booth on the opposite side. She leaned on her fleshy arms. "Gezzus, it's good to get off my feet. Two hours I been on and already my feet are aching." She ran a hand through her bleached hair. "Gosh, what a life." She twisted in the seat and looked back towards the counter. "Truckers," she said. "Best damn men on earth." She turned back to Norma. "Where ya heading?"

"West," Norma said.

"Any place special?"

Norma shook her head. "I'll know when I get out there," she said.

"Hollywood, I guess," the woman said reflectively. "Did the same thing myself when I was your age." She smiled. "I used to be a looker when I was your age." She placed both hands under her heavy breasts and lifted them. "I had 'em this big when I was a kid, and real firm too," she said. "And I didn't need anything to hold them up, just like you." Her face took on a wistful expression as she recalled the past. "I had grown men grabbing at me when I was twelve. I thought I could just bounce them around at Hollywood and Vine and I'd be a big star. I got into the movies all right. "But, what movies!"

Norma had finished the sandwich and she was lingering over the coffee, listening with fascination.

"Look, kid, I don't know nothing about you, but stay away from L.A."

"I wasn't thinking about ..."

The waitress went on without hearing. "Maybe it's the weather out there, I don't know, but all they think about is sex. No kidding. Believe me, I like a good go as much as the next, and I thought I'd had plenty by the time I was sixteen, but cripes, I never seen nothing until I hit L.A." She shook her head. "I never knew there was so many ways to do it. One time I was ..."

"Hey, Sally," one of the men called from the counter. "Make with some fresh Java."

The waitress lifted herself from the booth with a grunt. "You just relax, hon," she said to Norma. "I'll see that you get outta here." She shuffled to the opening in the counter. "How many?"

"All around."

"Mine's black."

Pulling three cups from the shelf next to the large coffee urn, she drew them full, and carried them to the three truckers at the end. She leaned across the counter to talk. One of the men slid off his stool and walked to the bubbling, multi-colored juke box against the wall. He inserted a coin and pushed the selector, and returned to his seat. The machine whirred into action and the music of a large orchestra filled the diner. After several bars of strings, the orchestra faded into the background and a tremulous, sexless voice crooned about love.

Norma listened, not hearing the words, but knowing that it was the same story of pure love—something that she was beginning to believe did not exist. She noticed that the waitress glanced her way, and then the three truckers looked at her. She met their glance, and they turned away, still listening to Sally the waitress.

Before the record ended, Sally left the men and came back to the booth. She sat down and leaned across. "You're in luck," she said. "Harry, there, is driving through to St. Louis tonight. He says that he'll take you along."

Norma looked at the woman and then up at the three men. She looked back to Sally and the indecision was plain on her face.

"You can trust, Harry," Sally assured. "I wouldn't go a block with the other two, but Harry's a good guy. He won't try any funny stuff."

Norma wasn't sure, but there didn't seem to be any choice. She couldn't stay in the diner, and no matter how long she did stay, she was going to leave on foot or with somebody. And if she left on foot, sooner or later she was going to have to hitch-hike, and it would be a man that picked her up. Couples just didn't pick up a girl on the road. This woman had been kind to her, and she seemed to know the drivers. At least she would be on her way. In St. Louis she could find some sort of a job and earn bus-fare for the rest of the way. "Are you sure he won't mind?" she asked.

"He'll be glad of the company," the waitress said. "What's your name?"

"Norma."

"Nice name. Finish your coffee. He'll be leaving when you're done." She got up from the booth. She patted Norma's arm. "And remember. Stay away from L.A." She shuffled away.

Looking back to the window and the hammering rain, Norma stared hard at her own face. It was a pretty face, dark eyes slightly slanted; smooth olive skin, and aquiline nose, and a full-lipped sensuous mouth. When the dark hair was dry and curling over her shoulders it was an exotic face to match the lithe young body. She wondered when the last time was that she was happy with the face and figure. She only seemed to remember the unhappiness these physical properties brought to her. A stirring at the end of the diner brought her head around.

The three men had risen and were moving towards the cash register. One of them separated and came towards Norma. A big, sandy-haired man, he wore a battered cap on the back of his head. He was dressed in chinos and blue shirt and a light jacket. He stopped by the booth and smiled. "I'm Harry," he said. "Sally said you'd like a lift to St. Louis."

Norma nodded, not sure what to say. He dug his hands into his pockets and rocked back on his feet. "I'll get my rig and bring it up to the door," he said. "You be ready to hop in and you won't get wet."

"All right."

He turned and walked away, stopping by the register. He handed some bills to the waitress, and went to the door. "Keep 'em on the road," he said to his two friends.

"Watch the white line," one of the two said.

He slid back the door. The sounds of the downpour came in from the night with a blast of rain. Harry ran into the rain, slamming the door after him.

Norma slid out of the booth and stood up. She stretched, aware that the two drivers were staring at her, she took her coat from the hook and draped it over her shoulders. Pulling it across her breasts, she went to the register. "Thanks a lot," she said to Sally.

"It ain't nothing," the waitress said.

"Sure you wouldn't rather go to Chicago?" one of the men asked, grinning.

"I'm sure, thanks!" Norma smiled. She was watching the window. When she saw headlights suddenly finger across the graveled lot in front of the diner, she went to the door. A big diesel roared into action and the lights swept across the windows. Norma gripped the door handle and pulled hard, sliding it aside. The driving rain smote her and she recoiled. The truck wheeled up before the door. Norma stepped into the rain and slid the door closed. The truck door was open and she ran, her head down. She jumped to the running board and a strong hand gripped her arm and pulled her inside. She twisted and dropped down on the high seat and pulled the door closed. She was breathing heavily and shaking the rain from her face.

"Wet out there!" Harry shouted above the roar of the engine.

"Terrible!" Norma was laughing. She threw the coat off her shoulders and settled back into the seat.

The diesel moved slowly over the crunching gravel. Harry was hunched over the big wheel, peering intently into the side mirror. He touched the macadam and settled back. The engine roared a protest and Harry jammed down on the clutch and changed gears. He picked up speed and shifted again, and then again, until the engine was a steady drone. The speed mounted.

It was comfortable in the cab and Norma felt good. Harry lit a cigarette and held the pack out to her. For the first time she remembered that she had left her purse in the last car, along with her cigarettes. She took one of Harry's.

"Thanks," she said. He handed her a lit match and she touched it to the cigarette and inhaled deeply. My only vice, she thought.

The windshield wipers flicked back and forth with studied monotony. The lights probed the dark and the rain seemed to drive at the speeding truck with relentless fury. The tires screamed on the wet blacktop.

"Where ya from?" Harry asked.

"New Jersey."

"Oh yeah? What part?"

"Trenton."

"Ah, nice town."

Yes, Norma thought, a nice town. Nice if you came from the nice part. Not so nice if you lived in a shack that was just waiting for the turnpike commission to tear it down. Not so nice if your neighborhood was full of hoodlums, and squalor seeped from every run-down hallway. Not so nice if your mother was a drunk and you had a stepfather who ....

"Got relatives in St. Louis?"

"No."

"How come you're going to St. Louis?"

"It's west."

West. The word sounded good to her. It had a clean quality to it. She had been thinking about it for a year. It was as far as she could go away from everything that she despised. The west meant California, and that was the color photographs in a copy of Holiday magazine that she had treasured and read until the pages were frayed. It was a land of smiles, a land of sunshine. It was her dreamland, the end of the rainbow for her, the one thing that had kept her going in her despair.

Her eyes were heavy. The steady drone of the engine, the wipers, the warmth of the cab, made her drowsy. Her head dropped several times and she fought to stay awake.

"Tired?"

"A little."

There's a place to sleep up back. Crawl up and catch forty winks."

Norma turned her head. Behind the seat was a full-sized bed.

"Go ahead," Harry said. "I'll holler if I need you to keep me awake."

Seeing the bed made her ache for sleep. Norma crawled over the back of the seat and stretched out on the narrow foam-rubber mattress. She burrowed her head into the pillow. The motion of the truck was pleasant. Lying there, she looked across Harry's broad shoulders at the road ahead disappearing under the lights.

CHAPTER TWO

Norma awoke with a start. The truck was stopped. Still sleep-drugged, she had a moment of fright, not quite sure where she was. She lifted herself on one elbow and brushed her hair from her face. The cab was empty. It was still raining.

A winking red light caught Norma's eye and she craned her neck to see through the windshield. It was a neon sign on a pole by the road. EATS, it blinked to the traffic in both directions, casting its momentary reflection on the wet road and the parking lot before the small, white lunchroom.

Leaning back, Norma closed her eyes and relaxed again. She was rested. She touched her dress and it was almost dry. She smiled to herself.

A door slammed and loud, laughing voices came above the sound of the rain. Norma heard running footsteps, then the truck door opened and Harry leaped in under the wheel, blowing and shaking the rain from his face. He turned to look back.

"You're awake," he said.

"Yes, I had a good sleep."

"Just a couple of hours. Lay back and take it easy." He turned the key in the ignition and pushed the starter. The engine turned over, sputtered and caught, rising to a roar and then settling down. Harry released the brake and pulled the shift into first. The truck began to roll.

"Where are we?"

"Just outside of Terre Haute."

The truck rolled on to the highway and Harry went through the laborious shifting until he had it down into fourth.

On her side, looking over Harry's shoulder, Norma watched the white line slide by. The night ahead was like an endless tunnel the truck was plowing through, confident that the road would go on and on.

Norma rolled on to her back and stared at the roof of the cab. Once again the motion lulled her and she closed her eyes and slept.

She awoke slowly, realizing in some recess of her mind that the motion of the truck had ceased. She opened her eyes, slowly at first, then with a snap. Her body stiffened and she was fully awake in a second. Harry's face was hovering over hers. She attempted to sit up, but his hand on her shoulder held her down.

"What ...?"

"Just take it easy," Harry said, smiling. He was standing on the seat, bent over and looking down at her. His hand moved away from her shoulder and he touched one of her breasts. "Nice," he said.

Norma struggled to get up. He touched her shoulder again, and with practically no effort he pushed her back.

"What are you doing?" Her voice was frightened and bewildered. She couldn't fully believe what her mind was telling her.

His hand covered her breast again. "No!" She brought both hands up and grasped his arm. Squirming away, she pressed against the back of the cab.

"Don't. Please, you're hurting me!"

"Just relax then." The smile was gone from his face. He brought his legs over the back of the seat and stretched out next to her, partially covering her, pinning her down.

"Let me go!"

"Take it easy, baby." Harry chuckled. He squeezed his fingers hard and Norma cried out in pain. She took her hands from his arm and he relaxed the pressure.

Norma's mind reeled with panic. There was no doubt what he was going to do. And he was too strong for her. She was helpless. She felt his hand slide inside her dress, felt the heat of fingers that encircled her breast. His big blond face came down over hers. She turned her head to avoid his mouth, and he kissed her on the neck, his lips hot and moist.

"Harry, please. Sally said you wouldn't do any-think like this."

He gave a short laugh. "Her!" he said, "I paid that bitch three bucks to Sally for the build-up."

Norma felt sick to the stomach. The waitress at the diner hadn't been asking the three drivers to help her, she had been selling her to the highest bidder. It's rotten! her mind screamed. This whole filthy world is rotten!

Harry took his hand away. He gave her a strange wondering look. She felt that he was going to stop. But he began to move the hand down over her body, tracing the curve of her waist, the flat plate of her stomach. Norma struggled, and screamed, but the sound was lost in the cab. She whimpered and closed her eyes tightly, keeping her face averted from his. Her mind was numb with terror. She felt his hand glide over her hip and down the outside of her thigh. He pressed hard against her. She gasped for breath. No man had ever been against her like that. Her body stiffened. She began to tremble.

It was warm in the cab. Harry was sweating and breathing heavily. He grasped the hem of her dress and pulled it up over her thighs. Norma crossed her ankles, but he forced his hand between her legs. She cried out.

Harry was releasing his belt. "Don't," she begged. "Please don't."

"Sorry, I just gotta!" He was wild, like an animal. "Relax kid. You'll like it. I'm good."

"No!" She began to cry. "Oh, dear god, please don't!"

Now he was over her, pressing down heavily, his breath hot on her neck, his weight full upon her.

She had many times imagined what this would be like, had always thought of it as a thing of beauty, a consummation of love. She did not know that it could be a horror. Helpless, she closed her mind to it. But as a sharp, tearing pain rocketed through her body she screamed, and screamed. Then her mind slipped into darkness.

She came to consciousness, remembering only the pain. She felt dirty. Harry was sitting behind the wheel, smoking. He looked back when she stirred. "You all right?"

Her dress was up to her waist and twisted under her. It was blood-stained. Norma pulled it down quickly. She glared at Harry and he lowered his eyes sheepishly.

"You shoulda told me," he grumbled, "I didn't know you was a damn virgin."

Norma could not speak. She slid her legs over the back of the seat and dropped down. A dull ache throbbed behind her eyes. Her right hand found the door handle. She looked across at him and spoke through her teeth. "Filth," she said, "that's what you are."

"Look, I'm sorry, I didn't mean to ..."

"Filth!" She jerked the handle and threw her shoulder against the door. It flew open and she tumbled out, dropping to the side of the road.

"Hey, wait a minute!" She heard him call.

The rain lashed at her. Dragging her coat, she slid down the slight embankment to a field. The weeds were wet against her legs. She ran, stumbling in the darkness.

"Where you going? You crazy?"

His voice drove her on. She plunged ahead, slipping in the mud. She fell, felt the wet reach her skin, struggled to her feet and kept running. Briars tore at her legs, clawed her dress. She caught her coat on a bush and it jerked her to her knees. She pulled it free and struggled up, still running into the night. The sobs wracked her body. She wanted to run until she died. Nothing could ever be any good again. Harry's voice was lost in the whip of the wind-driven rain, but he could never be far enough behind her. She tripped over a knoll and fell headlong into the tall grass. She had dropped her coat and she had to crawl about to find it. She went up the small rise on her hands and knees, and at the top she fell forward and cried, her fists clutched the grass, her face down, as though she were finding comfort in the bosom of the earth.

The sound of the diesel roaring into motion brought her head up. She looked back to see the headlights sweep out over the highway and then move off. She watched until the tail lights were out of sight, then she turned back and cried bitterly.

When she could cry no more, she pulled herself to her feet. It was too dark to see where she was. She threw the wet coat over her shoulders. She had lost one of her shoes. She kicked the remaining shoe off and began to walk slowly, moving away from the road. Reaching a tree that offered a little protection from the rain, she sat down, huddled against the trunk. She pulled the coat over her head and pulled up her legs.

Is this all there is? she asked herself. Isn't there somewhere that you can live without every man you meet trying to paw all over you? Does every woman have this? I know they don't. I know that women marry and live decent lives and have children and men that love them. Is there something wrong with me? Was I put on this earth just to be something to lay under a man?

The tears came again, her anguish heightened by the dark-ness and the rain.

Then, as before, her mind brought forth the picture of her particular west. She saw it now as something that could purge her of the evil she felt was deep within her. It soothed her and her body calmed.

The clean, country-grass, warm, wet odors came to her and she savored them. She pulled herself into a ball beneath the coat and slept.

CHAPTER THREE

A cock crowed somewhere. The morning birds chattered and fluttered, setting up a nervous cacophony. The trees whispered under a light breeze, the sodden branches dipping to loose the remnants of the rain from the leaves, the droplets rattling in their descent and exploding on the ground, spreading to glisten for one final moment in the sun before entering the insatiable maw of the earth.

Norma opened her eyes. She shuddered and hugged her arms tightly about her. Daylight had wiped away the terror of the night. Now she found it difficult to adjust her thinking to what had happened.

She heard an engine, the sound growing steadily until it resembled a hive of bees. She lifted her head and moved her eyes in the direction of the sound. A car appeared on the highway, the indistint figure of a man hunched over the wheel. The sunlight glittered on the glass. The sound reached a dull roar, like rushing water, then faded as the car passed on.

Shrugging the wet coat from her shoulders, Norma rubbed a hand over her face without realizing that the hand was muddy. Her legs were stiff and she twisted them from under her and stretched them. She shuddered again and sniffed. She rolled away from the shade of the tree and sat in the sun, pulling her knees up under her chin.

The strong rays of the early-morning sun were warm on her back and she could feel the blood begin to move more freely. With the new warmth, she now felt the dampness of the ground, and she got to her feet. Looking down, she wondered what had become of her shoes, then shrugged it off. She was a little over a hundred yards from the highway, in the center of a field. A slight steam was rising off the field, and the grass glistened, the tall weeds reflecting the many hues of yellow and red.

Stretching her arms over her head, Norma turned and looked behind her. The field was obviously part of a large farm. There was a stand of trees to the right and on the left, partially obscured by heavy brush, were several slant-roofed ramshackle buildings.

She had to get her clothes dried before she could set foot on the highway again. The thin cotton dress was plastered to her body like tissue, and she didn't relish the idea of wearing the wet coat in the gradually warming day. Turning, she started towards the run-down buildings, her steps dragging a bit, the weeds whispering against her legs.

At the edge of the field she stopped and listened. There was nothing but the sound of the birds and the throaty crowing of the distant rooster. She found an opening in the thick briars that fringed the field, and sidled through.

There were two buildings, one smaller than the other; the larger a one-time storage shed. The vertical board siding was grey with disuse, patches of scaling white paint attesting to a long-ago magnificence. Some of the boards hung askew, clinging to rusted nails. The door of the larger building hung on one hinge.

Norma spread her coat over a bush where the sun was directly upon it. She went to the door and pulled it aside. It groaned on the hinge, but moved easily. The grass was down before the door and she could see that the door had been moved recently. She paused reflectively, wondering if the farmer used the shed and when he might arrive. She shrugged, and stepped inside. The smells of musty hay and machine oil greeted her. Except for a roto-tiller in the corner and some tools leaning against the wall, the shed was empty. Looking up, she saw that there was a small loft, and a handmade ladder. Going to it, she climbed the ladder. There was enough room under the roof for her to stand upright. She went to the end of the loft and unlatched the door there, swinging it out. Light streamed in.

Reaching behind her neck, she unzipped the dress. She grasped the hem and pulled it over her head. She was suddenly conscious of her nakedness, but there were no prying eyes and she laughed lightly to herself. Shaking out the dress, she went to the door, leaned out and hung the dress on a nail outside.

There was nothing to do now but wait. She padded about the small loft. There was a half-used bale of straw against one wall. She went to it and sat down, leaning back and drawing her knees up. Now she began to wish for a cigarette and she realized that she was hungry.

She had no idea for sure where she was, but she knew that Terre Haute was near the Indiana border, and she must be in the next state. But she didn't know what state was next to Indiana. Somewhere in the mid-west, sitting in a barn naked. She knew that this should amuse her, but it was too serious to be funny.

For the time being there was nothing to do but wait until the dress was dry, but then what? She was a long way from California, and already her purse was gone, she had lost her shoes, and she was broke. She tried not to think about what else had happened, but it was impossible. Raped. She formed the word on her lips and said it quietly to herself, "raped."

She pressed her legs tightly together. God, how he had hurt her with his ripping blundering assault. She didn't remember everything, but she could vividly recall the tearing pain. The pain had only lasted a short while, not the way she thought it would be. Now she didn't feel anything.

Closing her eyes, she leaned her head back. Sunlight slanting through the openings in the boards fell across her. It felt good, and she stretched her shapely legs. She breathed heavily, deeply. Her large, jutting breasts rose and fell, the shaft of light across them turning the bruised violated nipples the color of copper. She ran her hands over the wide flare of her hips and sighed.

So I gave it up in the back of a truck, she thought, and that's what I've been fighting to keep since I was twelve. It hardly seems worth all the effort now. And that's why I left home. Three days ago. Three days! Is that all? Seems like a year. At least I'm glad I left. Nothing could be worse than that slimy…

Norma shuddered, remembering. She had been in bed, lying awake, when she heard her stepfather come into the house. He stumbled against a chair in the dark and cursed.

"Mike, that you?" The high whine of her mother.

"Who the hell'd you think it was, Cary Grant?"

"Wait a minute, I'll get up."

"Stay where y'are, you bag of bones." The voice was whiskey-harsh.

"Mike."

"Shaddup!"

"You'll wake Norma."

"Hah! Wake Norma. Do her good, that stuck-up little bitch." He banged across the room in the dark.

Norma tensed and listened, holding her breath. She saw the reflection of the light from her mother's room as it went on.

"Get back in bed or I'll bust ya in the mouth."

"Mike, please…"

"Shaddup!" There was the sharp crack of an open palm slamming against flesh and Norma's mother cried out sharply. Then there was the dull thud of a fist, a whimper, a scuffling of feet. "I told you to shut that mouth." Another slap, another, and then a body hitting the floor. A gasp as he kicked her and then the whimpering cry that became a gagging sob.

The footsteps were heavy on the floor, coming closer, the door to her room kicked open, the dark outline of the burly man framed in the half-light of the doorway. He entered the room, groping. He reached the foot of the bed.

"You're awake," he said. "You can't kid me. I know you're awake." He went to the wall and threw the light switch. He came back to the bed and stared down. Because of the heat of July, Norma was covered only by a thin sheet. She clutched it to her neck, but it stretched up to the sharp peak of her breasts and then fell away to touch the outlines of her body.

The step-father ran his tongue over his thick lips. He was unshaven and sweating and his tousled hair fell over his forehead. "We're gonna stop wasting that right now," he said. "I feed you, girl, and I put this roof over your head. And all the time you're putting it on the line for these wet-eared hotrod kids. Now, I'm gonna have a little." He tore the buttons from his shirt and pulled it off his arms. He came to the side of the bed. His fingers found the edge of the sheet and he tore it away. Norma was too terrified to cry out.

"Gosh. What a pair of knockers. An' I bin living in this house with 'em and never got my hands on 'em. I'm nuts." His eyes traveled to her thighs. and he grinned salaciously. "Little step-girl, you jest see what your ole daddy's got for you!" His hands were shaking as he tugged his belt loose.

"Mike!" Norma's mother was in the doorway, leaning on the jamb. "What in God's name are you doing?"

"Get outta here!"

"No! You can't! I'll call the police!"

He hesitated. He turned towards the doorway. "You call anybody, and I'll break you into pieces. Now, get your ass outta here. Unless you wanna watch!"

Norma's hand snaked out to the bedside table. Her fingers curled over a large jar of face cream. She swung her legs from the bed, twisting as she touched the floor, and raised the heavy jar over her head. He turned as she brought the jar down on the side of his head. He staggered back. His knees buckled and he went down.

Norma dropped the jar. She squirmed her feet into the shoes at her bedside, ran to the dress draped over a chair and pulled it over her head, tugging it down on her body as she ran from the room.

"Where are you going?" the mother wailed.

Without answering, Norma grabbed her purse and her coat, and fled from the house. Outside, she ran down street after street until she had to stop and slump against a building gasping for breath.

Three days ago! And now I'm ... where? Somewhere. At least I'm somewhere.

The sound of an engine interrupted her thoughts. It was not from the highway. It was a laboring sound and it came from another direction than the road. Norma leapt to her feet, went to the loft door and listened. The sound was approaching from across the fields. Besides the engine noise, there was an accompanying clatter. Then she saw it. A jeep was bouncing over a rutted lane with a flat trailer behind it. It was coming towards the shed and she could not reach her dress without being seen. She drew back.

Roaring as the wheels sild in the wet grass, the jeep came closer. Norma caught her breath, praying that it would go past without stopping. Brakes squealed in front of the shed and the engine idled.

"Wal, I'll be damned." She heard a man's voice. It had a youthful sound. "Somebody's coat on this bush." Silence and only the idling of the engine. Then muted footsteps, the scrape of weeds against boots. "Huh. Looks like a dress. Wal, I be go to hell, it is a dress." A short chuckle. "Them damned town kids. Horsing around in this old shed. Some high school kid must'a gone home bare-ass?" A longer chuckle, footsteps, then the door creaked back, Norma could hear the speaker inside the shed.

Shrinking back against the wall, she saw him go to the Roto-tiller in the corner and grasp the handles. He stopped and looked back and down. She heard his tongue click against the roof of his mouth and he released the machine. He walked out of sight and she heard him leave the shed.

Norma waited, her heart pounding, scarcely able to breathe. She heard him come back into the shed and then his boots scraped on the ladder. She saw his hands on the top rung and she pressed backwards, trying to cover herself with her hands. His head came up over the edge of the loft, slowly, the eyes wary.

There was a moment of dead silence, then his intake of breath was sharp. His eyes blinked and opened wide. "Wal, I'll be go to hell," he whispered. His shoulders appeared above the edge of the loft and he stopped there. He was young, about thirty, blonde-haired. His hands on the ladder were big and his shoulders strained the clean, white T-shirt. Norma felt the blue eyes covering her nakedness.

"What 'cher doin' here?" he asked, a slight catch to his voice.

"I...I..." she stammered, then burst out, "I was drying my dress. I got caught in the rain. I didn't know anybody would be here. I..." Her voice died. She moved back, harder against the boards, crouching to keep herself covered.

"Who are you?"

"I...I'm just passing through."

He scowled. "It's a damn strange place to be just passin' through."

Norma's face was desperate. "please, I just want to get dressed and get out of here."

"You ain't from around here at all?"

"No, I..." She stopped. He was smiling and he began to move slowly up the ladder.

"Please," she implored, "I'll leave."

"What's your hurry. I ain't gonna hurt you." He stood at the end of the loft, too tall to straighten without touching the roof, "I just came along for the tiller, there. Figured this was a good morning for a little light plowing." He emphasized the end of the sentence, smiling with insinuation. "Somebody bring you here last night and then leave without you?" He shook his head. "Can't understand some men. Now I'd never leave something like you just sitting around." He held up her coat. "This yours?"

Norma nodded. He spread the coat on the floor. "Sit down," he said. "Let's have a little talk." Norma saw the futility of trying to talk to him. He could only see her naked body and already there was a look of lust in his face. She was just a foot from the open doorway. It was about eight feet to the ground. She whirled suddenly. Grasping the edge of the door jamb, she spun out, wrenching her dress free from the nail. She heard the scrape of his feet as he came after her, and she jumped.

"Hey!"

She landed hard, the ground jarring her. She scrambled to her feet and ran.

"Wait a minute. I ain't going to ..."

Running wildly, Norma stumbled through a stand of bushes, the branches lashing at her.

"Damn it, girl, come back here!"

The thick wall of briars stood before her. She could not find the opening where she had come through. A sob caught in her throat. She saw where it was the least heavy, and flung herself on the sharp, clawing needles. Like a hundred grasping hands, the briars tore at her, searing her naked flesh. She pushed through, stifling the cries that rushed to her lips. The tears welled in her eyes and spilled over her cheeks. The pain was excruciating.

She burst through to the other side and the open field with a gasp of relief. Her body was a criss-cross of red scratches and angry welts. It felt as though she were on fire. She raced across the open field towards the highway.

A peal of raucous laughter reached her from behind. She turned her head to look back. The farmer stood with his hands on his hips, his blonde head flung back, laughing.

Seized by a combination of fear and fury, realizing that she must look comic dashing naked across the field in the morning sunlight, but also feeling trapped and helpless, Norma dropped to her knees in the grass. She clutched the dress to her pain-seared breasts and the sobs broke loose, shaking her shoulders and bowed head.

The bastards, she wailed, the dirty-minded bastards! Why can't they leave me alone? Sudden silence behind her was like a shot. She gasped and turned. He was coming through the stand of briars.

Norma leaped to her feet. He could still drag her back to the shed. She ran for the highway. He wouldn't dare take a chance on coming after her with the danger of a car coming by. She ran, shaking out the dress. She looked back. He had stopped. She hesitated long enough to pull the dress over her head. The sun had dried it sufficiently and it came over her easily. She ran on and scrambled up the bank to the highway.

A car was approaching. She waved her arms frantically. The car roared by, a couple in the front seat. The woman gave her a hard look.

Norma looked back across the field. The farmer stood unmoving. Her feet touched the warm black-top and she began to run again, as though in pursuit of the speeding car.

The laughter broke out again, following her. She kept running, her hair a wild tangle jouncing on her shoulders. The tears streamed down her face.

Leave me alone, she gasped, leave me alone, leave me alone!

CHAPTER FOUR

It was almost noon. The road was a shimmering black ribbon, flat and straight. It was warm under her feet, but not as bad as the gravel on the sides; when a truck passed and she had to leap off the road, dance over the hot gravel to stand tottering on the tufts of crab grass.

There were no shade trees; just scrub oak crawling near the ground and scattered alders, almost too thin to cast a shadow. The road was hemmed by fencing and beyond the fences were fields of wheat, parched and stately stiff, crackling under the intense heat. Occasionally there was a car-wide gate in the fence, and a short drive to the oil pumps that rose and fell with thumping regularity.

Norma stopped walking and shaded her eyes to look ahead. She saw a cluster of trees and the white spire of a church. A town. She licked her parched lips thoughtfully. She couldn't walk through a town. She had tried running her fingers through her hair, but it was still wild and unkempt. Her legs and arms were covered with scratches, and her dress was streaked with mud.

A car approached, and she came to her feet. She went to the edge of the road and waited. It was a black sedan, the sun reflecting from its shine. It was traveling fast. Norma forced a smile. Her heart was beating rapidly. She lifted her hand. When she saw that it was a man and woman in the car, she lowered her hand. The woman's eyes covered her as the car shot past.

"Whatta you looking at, you stuffy bitch!" Norma shouted, her pain and despondency rousing her anger. "You think I'm enjoying myself. You and your fat husband in your big car! The hell with you!" The car rushed on, unhearing.

The heat was too much. She was getting dizzy. Shimmering heat waves were rising from the highway and ahead of her it seemed to turn to water. She hated to think about going into the town looking the way she did, but she had to get out of the sun.

She began to walk, her steps dragging and her head bent. She could feel the sweat run down between her breasts, staining the dress at the waist. The salty perspiration covered the mesh of scratches and the pain made her whimper. Her head ached, the dull throb beating in time to her pulse. She closed her eyes and ragged balls of light danced against her eyelids. She found it hard to breathe. She knew that she was weaving in the road, but she could not control her legs. She began to stagger. Her legs gave way. She pushed her arms out to break her fall. The macadam was pillow-soft. She pressed her cheek to the warm surface.

From the far distance she heard the drone of an engine. She tried to move her legs, lift her shoulders. The effort was too great. She relaxed, sighing. The sound was louder, the clatter and chug of an old truck. Funny how she could almost tell an engine's age by the sound—she had heard so many. I don't care, she said, smiling, enjoying the lights that danced in her darkness. I don't care. Too tired. To t. .i. .r. .e. .d.

The screech of brakes, the mutterings of a man's voice, the slam of a metal door. Her senses still responded even though she was without the will to move, or live, or care.

"Whatta ya make of it, Dell?" A heavy, harsh voice. "She hit by a car?"

"I don't know." A female voice, husky and full-bodied, but lilting in the way of a woman.

"She dead?" The man's voice again.

Hands touched her shoulders, gripped her and pulled her over.

"She's smiling," the man said.

"She's alive. Her chest is moving."

"Yeah, and some chest it is, too."

"Cut it out, Gus, the kid might be hurt."

Norma opened her eyes. The sky swam overhead. The two figures over her were blurred and wavering. She moved her lips, but no words came.

"Must be the sun," the man said. "We better get her in the truck."

"Yeah, poor thing, she's really beat up. I'll get her legs."

Hands under her shoulders, lifting her. Suspended, the two people carrying her. She closed her eyes again.

"Put her feet down and pull the tarp aside," the man said. Her feet touched the ground. "Okay, you hold her up and get on the truck and pull her up."

She was rising, strong hands under her arms pulling her up. "Okay, Dell. I got her. Now hop up here and make a place for her."

They put her down on something soft. She opened her eyes again. "Get some water, Gus," the woman said. "And you better pull off the road for a few minutes."

She could see the woman's face faintly. Although she could not make out the features, she saw that the face was encircled with yellow hair. The truck lurched and rolled, then stopped. The man returned.

"Here y'are, Dell."

A cool cloth on her face, moving slowly. Gentle hands. The wet cloth moving over her neck and shoulders. Feels so good, want to sleep. Gently, soothing, cool, the cloth and the soft hands inside her dress, over and under her breasts.

"Want some help?"

"This is no time for jokes, Gus! This kid is sick."

"Just too much sun, I think. She'll come around in a few minutes."

Water poured on her forehead. So nice, cool. Her head ached, but it was clearing. She opened her eyes again. She saw the woman clearly.

"Feeling better, hon?"

Norma nodded weakly, tried to smile. "Better," she whispered.

"Here, take a little of this." The woman held a tin cup to her lips and a trickle of water entered her mouth, ran down her throat. "Hot," she muttered, then closed her eyes. "Sun ... so ... hot."

"You're okay now, hon. Just rest."

Norma felt better. The sun was no longer burning down on her, and she felt that she was in friendly hands.

"We better get rolling, Dell," the man said. "We gotta be in Bloomington tonight."

"Well, get rolling."

"What about her?"

"I'll stay back here with her."

"You mean take her with us? She probably lives around here. Hell, that's kidnapping, Dell."

Norma opened her eyes and her fright was mirrored in them. She fought for her voice. "Don't leave me," she gasped.

"You on the road, kid?" the blonde woman asked.

Norma nodded. "Please. Don't leave me ... here." Her head slumped back.

"Get her rolling, Gus. I know a kid on the run when I see one. Wasn't I on the move enough myself? Believe me, I feel for the kid."

"Whatta we gonna do with her?"

"Not what you're thinking, you old reprobate," the blonde said, laughing. "Just get that look outta your eyes and get driving."

The man chuckled and Norma heard him leave. She felt the woman's palm on her face. It was comforting and she slept.

Norma awoke to a swaying, bumping motion. She opened her eyes and her head was clear. She was alone. She looked about her, remembering. She was in the back of a truck, a tarpaulin beneath her. It was still light, semi-light inside the truck. Around her was piled strange equipment, folded banners and a number of wood and metal boxes. Everything was lettered with the same words: KIRKLAND'S WORLD OF WONDERS. It was some kind of a show.

Sitting up, she pressed her hands to her temples. There was just a trace of the headache. She recalled the man and the blonde woman, remembering the kindness they had shown her.

She leaned back against the tarp, thinking. What kind of people had picked her up? They must be show people. Remembering their friendly banter, she felt at ease with them.

The truck slowed down. She noticed the change as the tires left the road and ran on gravel. The brakes whined and the truck stopped.

"Piss call," a man's voice said.

"Gus, do you have to always say that. I hate talk like that, and you know it."

The man laughed and a door slammed. Then another door, and then footsteps on the gravel. Norma sat up. One corner of the end tarp was lifted and sunlight slanted into the truck.

"Hi, there." The blonde woman was smiling. "Feeling better?" She called over her shoulder. "Hey, Gus, our passenger is sitting up."

Norma smiled. "A lot better," she said. "You were awful kind."

"I'm the kind one." The man's face appeared, a toothless grin spreading the wide mouth. "I stopped the truck. Now if you're thinking of giving out some thanks, well I'll ..."

"Oh shut up, Gus." The woman jabbed him in the side and he leaped back.

"Don't do that! God-o-mightly, woman, you know I'm goosey."

The woman laughed. "Don't pay any attention to Gus. He's just getting old. How about something to eat?"

Norma hesitated. The mere mention of food made her ache. "I don't think I look …"

"You look like you been dragged for fifty miles," the woman said, "but that don't mean you're not hungry. C'mon, we ain't stopped at the Ritz."

"Well, I'm afraid that I don't …"

"So you're broke. Happens to everybody! C'mon! Gus can gawk at you over his coffee."

Norma climbed down from the truck. The man helped her down, then stood back. They were in the parking area surrounding a diner of the old trolley-car design. It was green and yellow, the paint faded and scaling around the windows. *Highway Grill* was lettered across the front in script.

"My name's Della," the blonde woman said, smiling to show her perfect white teeth. "This is Gus."

"Howdy."

"My name is Norma."

"Okay, Norma," Della said. "Let's chow down." They started towards the diner. "This gravel hurt your feet?"

"No, I guess I'm getting used to it."

There were no booths inside, just the counter and stools. The place was empty. Della led the way to the right and sat on the end. Norma sat next to her and then Gus.

A thin, bald-headed short-order cook in a grease-spattered T-shirt and apron stood in front of them.

"What's good?" Gus said.

"Everything's good before we put it on the grill," the counter-man said, grinning.

"How come they all say that?" Gus asked.

"They need an answer for the same dumb question," Della said. "I'll have the ground steak and french fries. And coffee."

"Same," Gus said. He looked at Norma, then added, "Make it three; and one milk." He winked. "Gotta build you up, Kiddo." He chuckled meaningfully.

"Some joke," Della sad. "A real comedian."

Norma smiled. She liked Gus. A mop of gray hair topped his round, freckled face. His eyes were dark blue and they sparkled, giving the widemouthed, pug-nosed face a mischievous look. There was a coarse tone to his humor, but it was so good-natured that Norma found it refreshing. She noticed a wedding ring on Della's finger. So the two were married. Della seemed younger, in her forties, and pretty. Large, round breasts pushed out against her blouse. A wide belt was cinched at her narrow waist and a flaring peasant skirt accentuated the wide hips.

"Where you heading?" Della asked.

"West."

"Just west."

Norma laughed uneasily. "I guess so. I really don't know anything about the west, but I was in the east and it seemed like the only way to go."

"Looks like you dropped a few things on the way," Della said.

Norma started, thinking of Harry and the night in the rain, then she realized that Della meant her shoes. "Yes."

Della clucked her tongue and scowled. "A girl by herself is always leaving somebody or something in an awful hurry," she said. "You're awful green, or you wouldn't have forgotten your purse. A woman is lost without her purse."

Norma laughed. "It's the first time I've been away from home."

"I won't ask you why you left. I can imagine. I remember how I left."

They fell silent while they ate. Norma was famished. She had to restrain herself from bolting the food. When she was finished, she felt alive.

"Smoke?"

"Ohhhh, yes. I'd almost forgotten that I smoked."

She took one of Della's cigarettes and Gus held the light for her. She gulped the smoke and let it out slowly. "I feel wonderful," she said.

"How old are you?" Della asked.

"Eighteen."

"Ever do any dancing?"

"You mean regular dancing?"

"Well," Della said, "I meant show dancing, but if you can do ballroom dancing, you can learn the other."

"I do most of the dances you do in school," Norma said. "Rock and all that."

"Well," Della said, "if you're not in too big a hurry to get out west, maybe we can find you a job."

"A job?" Norma's eyes lighted and Della laughed.

"We're with a carney," Della said. "The Kirkland Show. I run the mitt camp and Gus is a talker for the ten-in-one. It's not a bad life and I think we can find you a spot. Interested?"

"Well... well, I mean... oh, yes!"

"A deal." She held out her hand and Norma grasped it. "What do you say, Gus think she'll make a carney?"

"Well," Gus laughed, "if you ain't got a pair of shoes to your name, you're about ready to join the carney. Welcome aboard." He held his hand out to Norma. She gripped it. The tears welled in her eyes, but she smiled back at his grinning face.

"Pay the man and let's get outta here, Gus," Della said. "We gotta be in Bloomington tonight. We're late already and Ed Kirkland will be having a fit."

"The old bastard'll foam at the mouth when he sees what we brought him," Gus said, sliding off the stool.

CHAPTER FIVE

It was night when they pulled into Bloomington. Della was asleep, her head against the window. Norma sat in the middle, pressed close to Gus, staring ahead.

Pulling up at a stoplight, Gus leaned from his window and called to a man on the corner. "Which way to the Fair Grounds?"

"Two blocks and turn right," the man shouted back. "Then just keep going."

The light changed. Gus pulled the shift down, grinding until it meshed. The truck rolled again. They made the turn, left the business district, passed through the screen-porched-white-house sections, then the asbestos-shingle section, and the no-paint-leaning-screaming-kids section; then across railroad tracks, then houses with fences and big yards, and bigger yards until it was fields, then the sky-lit blaze of light ahead on the right.

"I swear to God," Gus said, "You could put every damn town in the mid-west into one and there wouldn't be a bit of difference. If I didn't know better, I'd say that some lunatic went around with a set of plans and sold every town council on the same idea. You'll see. We play Kankakee after this fair, and that damn town will be a small version of this one."

"California is different," Norma said, remembering the photos in the Holiday magazine.

"Parts of it," Gus said. "Along the coast and in the mountains. But the towns and cities in the valleys are just like this one. Damndest thing. Americans think these housing projects are new. Hell, this whole country is one spread out project—all the same. I never seen a people so hopped up on scenery, and so eager to mess it up with these ugly towns."

Norma laughed. Della grunted and lifted her head. She yawned and rubbed her eyes.

"We're here, baby," Gus said.

"Happy days," Della grunted.

The Bloomington County Fair Grounds occupied the bare acres to the right of the road. For fifty-one weeks of the year it was as still and empty as a ghost town. Tonight it was blossoming for its six days of splendor.

Gus braked the truck and rolled off the highway, coming into the sweeping drive and the two white pillars of the main gate. He shifted down and stopped next to the guard box. "Where's the carney setting up?" he asked the uniformed guard.

"Bear to your left there. You're in the back."

"Thanks."

They drove slowly, passing the brightly lighted exhibit halls, then behind them, and around, and finally into the large brown-grass plot and the identical red trucks and the howls and curses of the carney going up.

A long horseshoe was being formed. The ferris wheel at the end was already towering against the night sky and the electricians were clambering over it. The roustabouts were laboring the top of the ten-in-one into place, sweating and wrestling the ropes as the boss canvasman bellowed and cajoled. Sledges rang on iron spikes. The Motordrome grew on the metal platform. Loose sidewalls flapped in the slight breeze. The flat joints were going up, crowding together along one side, the owners sorting their cartons of slum and mounting the wheels that would fleece the customers the next day. The merry-go-round made a trial run, the Wurlitzer Military Band Organ grinding out the chimes and the snare and the bass to the rowdy tune of "Tempest of the Heart," the painted horses plunging riderless, to the snort of the Ford V-8 motor. The banners were going up. The House of Mirth, The Seventh Wonder of the World, Maney's Merry Minstrels, Win, Win, Free, Free, The Only One, The Greatest—a gaudy splash of color under the white glare of the arc lights—The Wall of Death, Speed Lamston, The Fish Girl, Harry the Pinhead Boy, Girls, Girls, Girls.

"Where the hell you been?"

"Trouble with the carburetor," Gus shouted, shutting off the engine.

"I'll bet. Sleeping down the line more like it."

"Fat chance. Dell can't stay away from the smell of popcorn," Gus retorted. He heaved his door open and jumped down. Della opened her door. "C'mon, honey, I'll take you over to meet Ed Kirkland. He owns this rattrap."

Norma jumped from the truck after Della and followed her long stride across the grass. She was trying to look at everything, the excitement rising within her. It was thrilling. The din, the confusion, the good-natured shouting of laborers. Whistles followed their progress.

"Get a good look!" Della shouted.

"Wow, Dell, who's your friend?"

"Some action!"

"Drown in your sweat!" Della hooted.

"I could drown in that," someone cried, and people laughed.

Della stopped and whirled. Her eyes flashed. She glowered at the group of men who were roughnecking the canvas. They lost their grins under her angry stare. She walked slowly towards them, then stopped with her hands on her hips. "Who said that?" she snapped.

The men shifted and looked at one another. "I can imagine," Della said, picking out the smallest of the group. "You haven't got the guts of a pissant, Barnes. You're all mouth and hog swill."

"Aw, Dell," the wrinkled little man said, flustered, his face turning red, "I didn't mean nothin'."

"You never mean nothing, Barnes. To me you don't mean nothing at all anyhow. But don't you say anything more to me, and don't ever say another thing to that girl, or you'll be back in the gutter where you came from." Turning away from the silent looks of embarrassment, Della walked back to where Norma was waiting.

"There's some people that can't say anything without it being dirty," Della said. "C'mon, kid."

There were no more catcalls. They passed the row of growing flat joints and Della waved and greeted all the men and women who worked inside the counters, setting them up.

The pay-wagon and office was a large truck set back from the midway on the right. Steps led to a small platform and the door. Della knocked.

"Come in."

Della opened the door. She stepped inside and Norma followed her. It was a small, crowded room. A bulky man with a round, florid face and no hair sat behind a cluttered desk in the corner. There was a file cabinet bolted to the wall. A small table with an adding machine, a bench running along the side opposite the doorway. Shelves and pigeon-holes surrounded the grilled window at one end. A heavy, brass-haired woman stood at the shelves, counting a wad of bills. She turned and the man at the desk looked up, his cigar tilting.

"Hiya, Della," the man said, "You just get in?"

"Yeah, we had a little engine trouble."

"Bad?"

"No. Gus fixed it himself. Hello, Pearl."

"Hi, Dell," the woman said.

Their eyes turned to Norma who was standing by the doorway. "Ed," Della said, "This is my cousin. Name's Norma."

Ed Kirkland looked over his desk and down at Norma's bare feet. "Right out of the hills, eh? A real Daisy Mae!"

Della smiled. "She lost her shoes."

"Running to find her Aunt Della, no doubt," Kirkland shifted his cigar. His eyes narrowed.

"Well, uh, the fact is, Ed, I ..."

"You found a stray cousin on the road and you want me to give her a job."

Della grinned. "Now, Ed. You ought to be running the mitt camp yourself. This little girl ..."

"How old are you, Norma?" Kirkland interrupted.

"Eighteen," Norma said, her voice shaking.

"Wouldn't be closer to sixteen," Kirkland said.

"No." Norma said quickly. "I was eighteen three months ago."

Kirkland nodded slowly. "Well, you sure look eighteen. Whatta you do?"

"Do?"

"She's a dancer," Della said.

"Are you?"

"Well ... I ..." Norma looked to Della for help.

"Hell, Ed, stop giving the poor kid a hard time. She's a good kid and she needs a job. She's young and she's got a good body. She could just stand there and look better than those bags you've got in the girl show. I'll teach her to dance."

"Why didn't you say that in the first place?" Kirkland said, his eyes twinkling, the cigar making circles. "Okay, Norma, let's see what I'm buying."

Norma hesitated, swallowing hard. She looked at Della, then back to Kirkland. "Wh ... what do you mean?"

Kirkland laughed. "C'mon, I'm not just a dirty old man. I want to see your body without the dress."

"It's okay, kid," Della said. "If you're gonna be a stripper you'll be showing it to plenty of people. He daren't lay a hand on you while Pearl's around."

The brass-haired woman chuckled. "You're among friends, Kid."

Stripper. The word was like a shock to Norma. It had not occured to her that dancing with a carnival would mean stripping. She should have realized, of course. What other kind of dancing would a carnival feature. The idea was too new to her, and she didn't believe that she could actually bring herself to take off her clothing in public.

"No need to get embarrassed with me, kid," Kirkland said. "I gotta see what I'll be selling to the public. Too many chicks come here with a forty-inch bust that turns out to be foam rubber."

She wanted the job. She had to have it. What was she going to do to get to California? She was ready to do a lot worse just for a ride back there on the highway. This, at least, was a job. Her hand went to the zipper at the back of her neck. Norma's fingers stopped there, but she forced them to pull the metal fastener down. She bent over and grasped the hem of the dress. She pulled it over her head, wriggling out of it, then stood straight! Naked as she was born, unmoving, the dress hanging in her hand.

Kirkland leaned forward. He took the cigar from his lips and came slowly to his feet. "Gosh kid!" he muttered. "What the hell happened to you!"

Della's breath came in sharply. The three people stared at the criss-cross of briar wounds. Norma took a step back. "I … I fell in some briars," she said. Kirkland's eyes were questioning, and Norma knew he wondered what she was doing in the briars naked. "A man was chasing me. He tried to rape me," she blurted, the words tumbling from her trembling lips. "I was out in the rain all night and I was drying my dress and he saw me and came after me and he was going to … to …" Her voice faltered and tears brimmed in her eyes.

Ed Kirkland stepped forward. His hands gripped her shoulders. "Easy there, kid," he said, his voice gentle. He stepped back. "That must have hurt," he said. He whistled softly. His eyes covered her slowly and he shook his head. "She can't go in the show like that." He reached out and ran a finger over a gouge on one of her breasts. "I don't know, Dell."

"Aw, it's not that bad," Della said. "Those scratches will mostly be gone in a week, and the rest we can cover with make-up."

"Well, I don't know." Kirkland rubbed a hand over his bald head.

"Try to see that body without the scratches, Ed," Della said. "With her on the bally platform you wouldn't even need a talker."

"I think she's right, Ed. You don't find something like that everyday," Pearl said.

Kirkland went back to his desk and stood there rubbing his chin. "Okay," he said, smiling. "Okay. Get that dress back on, quick. I'm not that old."

"How much?" Della said quickly.

"What?"

"How much do you pay her?"

"Dammit, Della, you oughta be a shill. First you're weeping all over the place to get me to hire the chick and now you're getting hard about money. She can't even work yet."

"How much?"

"Fifty a week."

"Seventy-five."

"What? You outta your head? Fifty."

"Seventy-five, and only because she can't dance yet."

"Sixty."

"No."

"Aw, okay, okay." Kirkland clapped a hand to his forehead and grimaced. "Seventy-five, starting next week."

"And fifty for signing on," Della made snapping noises with her fingers. "She has to get some shoes."

"I'm paying her to take her clothes off, not put them on," Kirkland lamented.

"Damn it, Ed, why do you have to do something nice, then louse it up with your penny-pinching?" his wife said.

"Whaaaat?"

"This kid will make you rich, for Pete's sake. But she needs shoes."

Kirkland lifted both hands over his head in a gesture of despair. "Okay, okay. Cripes, why did they ever allow women to come in the Carney in the first place?" He shook his head and snorted. "Okay, Pearl, give the kid the fifty and get a chit signed." He turned on Della. "If she turns out to be a nine-day wonder, I'll get that fifty out of you."

"You'll be thanking me," Della said, smiling.

Pearl handed the bills to Della, and Norma signed her name to a receipt.

Della opened the door and Norma stepped out ahead of her. Turning back, Norma said, "Mr. Kirkland?"

"Uh?"

"Thank you." The gratitude in her voice was a husky tremor.

Ed Kirkland blinked. "I expect to get it back," he blustered, not trusting the sudden feeling of compassion he felt for the girl, shying away from the doe-like look of her eyes.

Della closed the door and they went down the steps. The noise around them was a steady clamor. "Okay," Della said, "Now I'll find you a place to sleep." They started for the lot beyond the wall of canvas, where a collection of house trailers were scattered without any apparent design.

"Gus and I share a trailer with Marge and Lew Hopper," Della said. "They run the snake show. We cut the expense of the trailer, and they haul around so me and Gus can handle one of the trucks and pick up a little extra. We keep the nut down that way. Not a bad deal, except if we run into chilly weather Marge takes her boa to bed with her to keep it warm, and that gives me the creeps. Holy cow, I've done my share of sleeping around, but that's too much."

A group of children were playing *Lie Low Sheepie* around the trailers, their voices sing-songy, melodious in the soft, warm darkness. The grass was higher here, and coarse under Norma's feet, but it was warm and she was beginning to enjoy going barefoot, something she had never done in the city. Cows moaned in the stock barns—their lowing a plaintive sound. The prize bulls answered, their bellows rich with emotion.

"Listen to that?" Della commented, laughing, as they walked. "I was raised on a farm in Carolina. When I was a kid and we heard that we used to sneak into the barn and turn the cow out into the pasture with the bull." She chuckled. "That was really a sight. Ever see a bull do it? He sure tears himself off a piece!"

Norma shook her head, embarrassed, but fascinated at the same time.

"Probably a damn good thing," Della said. "Makes sex with human beings seem like pretty weak stuff. I didn't stop envying that cow until I met a lumberman out in Oregon. Wow! I swear to God, I thought he had brought his axe handle along with him." She laughed, her voice rising. "Then I started feeling sorry for the cow, and I was damn glad to settle for a worn out old stud like Gus."

Della was still laughing when they reached a long silver trailer. "This is Darla Downs' trailer. She's with the girl show. I think you can shack with her." Della knocked.

"Yeah, okay," a voice said from within. "Keep your shirt on."

They waited a minute, then the door opened and the light from within flooded over them.

"Oh, hiya, Dell." Darla was a plump girl with a round face and orange hair. There was disappointment in the face. One hand held a flowered cotton wrapper closed, and when she saw who it was, she took her hand away and let the wrapper fall open. "C'mon in." She stepped back, her sagging breasts bouncing as she moved.

One end of the trailer held a fold-back table that was now down; two benches next to it, and a fold-away sofa bed that was now a sofa. Norma had never seen the inside of a trailer before and she marveled at the compact comfort. At the opposite end was a full-size bed, and between was a small kitchenette, closet and shower.

There were two beer cans on the table, an ash tray filled with butts and a folded copy of a confession magazine. Darla dropped down on one of the benches. She waved a hand at the sofa. "Put it down there," she said. "Golly, ain't it hot." She picked up a hankerchief and wiped the sweat droplets between her breasts.

"This is Norma," Della said.

"Hiya. How about a beer?"

"I could use one," Della said. "Feels like I got half the state of Illinois in my throat."

Darla lifted herself from the bench, grunting. She went to the small refrigerator. "How about you, kid?"

"I don't drink," Norma said, hesitantly. "I mean, I never did."

Darla stopped with the door open and arched an eyebrow. "You kiddin'?"

"I got nothing against it," Norma said, pleasantly. "It's just that I never … well, I mean if someone asked me to drink it was always some boy who wanted to … well, you know."

Darla's sudden laugh was throaty and it shook her long, heavy breasts. "How I know!" she exclaimed. "First time I got plastered was after a high school football game. There was a dance in the school gym and the bottle was hidden in the infirmary. While everybody was dancing, I took on the whole first team and the assistant coach. I sobered up about the time they were going to send in the scrub team." Her deep laugh was a bellow. "Funniest damn thing. I was laid out on this cot and didn't even know my name, but suddenly I come to and sit up and there's this little piss-ant of a kid tugging at his pants, never had it before and scared to death. 'What the hell you think you're doing?' I shout. He didn't say anything, just turned and ran." She laughed again, bringing the beer from the refrigerator. "How well I know!" She put the cans on the table and punched holes in the tops. "They get me drunk, screw me so bad I can't hardly walk, and of course I'm the one gets thrown out of school for being immoral." She handed a can of beer to Della and one to Norma. "Here, might as well get started among friends." She returned to the bench and sat down, leaning against the wall and putting one leg up before her. "Yessir, this is a great old world, all right. Just great!" She lifted her beer and took a deep swallow. "What's your racket, kid?"

"She's gonna dance with the show," Della said.

"I feel for ya," Darla said. "Though I guess it ain't so bad. You hustle on the side?"

"She's just gonna dance," Della said firmly. She gave Darla a hard look.

"You can starve to death that way," Darla said philosophically. "You stripped before?"

"No I haven't."

The girl arched her brow again. "Whatta ya got here, Dell, the original virgin?"

"A girl who needs a job," Della said. "And a place to sleep," she added. "That's why we're here. I figured since Shirley left, she might bunk in with you."

"Why not? After we open I don't sleep much here anyway." She laughed again. "Unless I get a customer or two between shows."

"You're gonna be a great influence on her young mind, I can see." Della said dryly.

"Aw, I'm not so bad. What else ya gonna do? Me, I like men. That's why I'm a lousy stripper. Ya gotta hate men to be a good stripper. You see their faces down there hanging out, their tongues dripping like a bunch of dogs, and you hafta want to taunt them with what you got, saying to yourself, 'Look at it, look at it, aint it nice. And you'll never touch it.' Me, I just grind it around and keep my eye out for a sport. I just advertise what I can do after the show. You can't be a good stripper that way. You hate men, kid?"

"No, I don't," Norma said quietly.

"That's too bad," Darla said, "but you will, believe me." She finished off her can of beer, letting it gurgle down her throat. She got up and went to the small refrigerator for more.

Della got to her feet. "I gotta get over and see how Gus is doing setting me up," she said. "Take care of her, Darla, but not too good."

"Hell, I'm just jealous," Darla said. "Sometimes I get to thinking what it might have been like if I hadn't gone to that damn football dance."

CHAPTER SIX

A light drizzle was falling and the morning was muggy. Norma had her hair tied back with a ribbon and she felt very young as she ran across the field, the dampness cool against her face.

She had slept well after sitting up and talking to Darla for several hours and drinking three cans of beer. She liked Darla. The girl made no secret of the fact that she was a prostitute, and that dancing with the carnival was just a good way to keep on the move and maintain a steady supply of men. Her name was actually Harriet Kutzner. But Norma had enjoyed their long talk, even though it was mostly a clinical discussion of sex with Darla doing the discussing.

The carnival was ready for the day's business. Norma came off the field into the midway. She saw Ed Kirkland, in a slicker and battered hat, standing by the pay-wagon talking to the boss canvasman. She slowed to a walk, and he shouted. "Keep running, kid. You'll get your pretty butt soaked. That's the cook shed right over there." He was smiling and Norma smiled back. She couldn't recall when she had felt so good. She ran across the deserted midway and ducked under the flaps of the tent Kirkland had indicated.

There were three long, rough wooden tables with benches, and the portable kitchen at one end. The three tables were filled with people hovering over their trays, eating, talking, some smoking.

"Morning, kid," Della called. "Get a tray over there and Carl will fix you up with some grub."

With all the eyes on her Norma felt uneasy, but she smiled back at Della and went to the portable stove where a tall, thin man was breaking eggs on the griddle. She took a tray from a pile.

"How ya have 'em, girlie?" Carl asked.

"Well, uh …"

"Over easy?"

"Yes, that'll be fine."

"Bacon? Home fries?"

Norma nodded and stood there waiting. The breakfast appeared on a plate and Carl slid it onto the tray. "Coffee?"

"Please."

"Hmmm. Don't hear that word much around here. Where you come from?" He smiled as he put the steaming cup on the tray.

"Over here, kid," Della said. "Move it over, Gus."

Norma sat between Della and Gus. She ate without talking, but her eyes moved about her, looking at everyone, returning some friendly smiles.

There was a girl with no arms, a pretty girl who ate directly from her plate, and did it in a dainty way that was intriguing. There was the tattooed man who looked like a magazine illustration and kept winking to make the figures on his cheeks dance; the fat woman who occupied two places and talked about her diet while she ate six eggs; The pinhead, a skinny man with a head that came to a peak, who grinned and spilled his food; the Half-man, a pleasant, blonde-haired youth who sat on the bench with his useless legs tied in a knot. And there were the midgets, two of them; a tiny woman who seemed perfectly formed and her mate, a large-headed mite with a high querulous voice and a constant scowl.

When she finished eating, Norma was introduced to the group at the table. Then she left with Della.

"Might as well get started with the dancing lessons," Della said. "It'll be another hour before anything opens in town."

They crossed the midway to the tent that was bannered in red and white: Girls, Girls, Girls, The Fabulous Follies. It was semi-dark inside, but Norma could make out the poles supporting the canvas and a five-foot platform.

"I'll get some light," Della said. She went behind the platform and a battery of lights went on, directly over the platform shining down. It was like a prize-fighting ring without the ropes. A ramp ran from the platform, up at an angle, to an opening in the rear of the tent.

"This here's the stage," Della said. "That's all there is to it. The marks stand around it." She put her hands on the stage and jumped up. "C'mon, I'll give ya a hand." She took Norma's hand and pulled her up, then she led the way up the ramp. "You come down the ramp and then do your dance. Back here there's a platform to wait on and steps." She pulled the flap aside and went through. "This is the dressing room. Nothing much, but it does the trick and it's better than some shows have it where you stand outside and get eaten alive by mosquitos while you wait to come on." She waited until Norma had a chance to look over the makeshift dressing tables. "Okay, let's go, I'll show you how to walk." They went back into the tent and Norma stood in the middle of the platform while Della took her place at the end of the ramp.

"You got music, see," Della said. "You come through the flap and just stand here. The talker announces you. You give it a big smile and lift your arms up. Give it a good pose and keep the arms up because that gets the knockers up higher. Then you come down like this, taking short steps and swinging your hips almost all the way around." She reached the platform. "Get it? Okay, give it a try."

Norma went to the end of the ramp and turned. "Okay," Della said, "the music. Give it a smile." Norma smiled and lifted her hands straight up. She posed. Della hummed a tune and Norma began to walk down the ramp, swinging from side to side. Before she reached the platform a loud, raucous laugh filled the tent. She stopped. The lights blinded her and she could not see into the depths of the tent.

"Whatta you want, Beethoven?" Della snarled.

"She walks like she's stepping over piles of cow dung," a man's voice answered.

Norma shaded her eyes to see and a figure approached the platform.

"Why don't you go beat your tom-tom?" Della said.

"I only want to help."

"I'll bet you do. You mean you heard that there was something new around."

"Cheese it, Della." The new comer was standing by the platform below Della. His eyes were on Norma who was still standing on the ramp. He was tall and well-built, a young man with a handsome, square-jawed face and a wide smile. His thick black hair was waved and unruly, giving him a bad-boy look, and his dark eyes were piercing. Norma felt herself trembling under his stare.

"Aren't you going to be polite and introduce us, Dell?" he asked.

"I'd rather throw her into the box with Lew Hopper's cobra," Della said.

The young man jumped onto the stage. He held out his hand, smiling, "I'm Lee Harker," he said. "What's your name?"

"Norma."

"Norma what?"

It suddenly occured to Norma that he was the first one in the carnival to ask her last name. No one else seemed interested. "Norma Chiari," she said.

"Italian?"

"Yes."

"My mother was Italian. That makes us piasanos." He smiled warmly, and Norma found herself reacting to his personality. "I have the combo that plays for this freak show," he said. "I play the drums. Go up there and come down again."

"Oh, brother," Della said, "now Beethoven's a director."

"I have to watch those stupid broads enough," Lee said. "I'd like to see one that's a dancer. Go ahead, Norma, I'll show you what to do."

Della lapsed into an angry silence, Norma went slowly to the end of the ramp and turned. Lee jumped down from the stage and uncovered his drums. He sat down and took the sticks in his hands. "Now then," he called. "I'm going to give you a beat on the tom-tom. Wait a minute, loosen your hair. Yes, that's it. Fine. Okay. Now, on the first beat, throw your head back and shoot your hands up like you're reaching for something." He hit the drums hard and Norma threw her hands into the air. "Stand on your toes! Okay, take one step with the right foot." He hit the drums. "Bend you knees! Throw your head down and reach for the floor." She followed the directions. "Arms back, fingers spread. Jerk your head up! Good. A step with your left. One hand straight out! Fine." He kept up the throbbing, stacatto beat, shouting the directions that transformed the short walk on the ramp into a sort of native rite. "Bare your teeth like you're starving and see a steak. Great! That's it." He brought her along slowly and Della found herself staring with fascination.

When Norma reached the platform Lee stopped the drums. He came and stood by the platform. "Try it like that a few times and you'll have something." He grinned at Della, and patted her cheek playfully. "Take over, coach," he said. Then he turned and walked out of the tent.

Norma was shaking. Her pulse still beating to the tempo of the haunting drums. She knew that she had come down the ramp, but she did not remember the walk. She had been carried away by the beat, her senses dulled by the primitive rhythm until her body had moved on its own. Stilled now, she was frightened by the realization of the wanton abandon she had experienced in the dance.

"There goes the world's prize bastard," Della said through her teeth.

Norma blinked with surprise. She was about to say something, but Della waved a hand and interrupted her. "I know, he seems so nice. Bastards always do. And he knows what he's talking about. That sonovabitch could make a penguin act exotic. Some of 'em don't always know what they're talking about, but they're bigger bastards when they do."

"I don't understand."

"You probably wouldn't. But take my advice and watch that sharpie like a hawk. Don't let him get his hands on you, or you're a dead duck. C'mon, that's enough for this morning. Let's borrow Marge Hopper's car and go get you something to wear."

They took the car, a vintage Chevvy, and drove into Bloomington. Della had an eye for bargain shopping. They managed to stretch the fifty dollars into low-heeled shoes, slacks, two blouses, and underwear. When they got back, the Fair was open, with speech ceremonies in progress at the grandstand, and the slack-mouth gapers filing up to the ticket box.

Della parked the car and put the keys in the trailer. They walked to the midway. Around them the Carnival was slowly grinding into motion.

"They'll be making a bally for the ten-in-one pretty soon, so I better get my tail in gear. Just look around and enjoy yourself, kid. Catch my act if you can, and see the girl show a couple of times. Holler if you want anything. I'll be around." She walked away and Norma moved slowly around the horseshoe set-up, feeling everything, trying hard to belong.

The eary morning drizzle had left and the sun hung in the pale, cloudless sky, slanting and drying, throwing long shadows. The loudspeakers brayed their scratchy, martial tunes.

Norma walked the length of the midway, past the ticket-taker and out through the heavy metal arch. She walked about twenty yards then turned and looked back. The big sign forming the top of the arch read: KIRKLAND'S WORLD OF WONDER. Beyond her the small canvas city stretched out and the skeleton of the ferris wheel loomed over everything.

"This is my home," she said aloud. "And this is the first time I have ever felt at home." With a quick shudder she remembered her mother and her odious, drunken step-father. Her own father had only been a yellowed photograph, a bricklayer who died in a building collapse before she ever saw him. "This is my home," she said again, shutting off the past.

She began to walk quickly, long-striding, her legs rubbing against the smooth gabardine of the black slacks. She put her shoulders back and her breasts strained against the white cotton shirt. She passed through the arch, smiling at the ticket-taker. She walked past the lunch concession and smell of hot-dogs and the pink cluster of cotton candy and the hot butter smell of popcorn. She paused at the cat-rack and the too-painted woman behind the counter returned her smile and said, "Hi. Saw ya in the cookshack for breakfast."

"I'm gonna be in the kooch show," Norma said, suddenly feeling confident speaking in the carny lingo.

"Just don't throw it outta joint," the woman said. "My name's Betty. Wanta try a couple of throws?"

"I'm Norma. I'd love it." She took three of the *nickle rockets* and aimed at the stuffed cats sitting in a row before her. She threw and missed. The woman laughed. "It's a good gaff," she said. "That fringe on the edges makes the cats look bigger. You gotta be Dizzy Dean to knock 'em off."

"See ya around," Norma said, laughing and moving off. She stopped before the PHOTO FOUR POSES TAKE IT YOURSELF and looked at herself in the mirror. Her black hair was pulled tightly off her forehead and tied at the back with a ribbon. It formed a frame for the perfectly moulded face, accentuating the sultry tilt of her eyes, the wide slash of her mouth. She took in all the features of the face and for the first time she enjoyed the fact that it was unusual and exotically beautiful.

The crowd was beginning to sift through the gate and mill on the midway, men and women with children in tow; pony-tailed girls with giggles and eyes for the sport-shirted boys who strutted and lounged in front of the games of chance, eager to show off and unaware that they couldn't win. Fat women, skinny women, men with bellies hanging over wide belts, laughing, scowling, gawking.

"Hiya, hiya. Here y'are, step right up ladies and gentlemen and see the wonders that will make the eyes pop and the heart stop. Nothing like it will ever appear on your teevee screen. Yes, yes, look here, look, look, right this way for the greatest collection of natures mistakes, novelty entertainments, marvels and curiosities." Gus was working up the first bally of the afternoon, his hawkish voice bawling out from the portable speaker in his hand. He waved his hands towards the gaudy banners and sang the praises of the ten-in-one, the sweat rolling off his forehead. "H'yar, h'yar, see the seal girl, the bee-ooo-ti-ful girl with flippers instead of arms and leggs, see the human pin-cushion, see Harry the pinheaded boy, all inside, step right up here, h'yar, h'yar."

A crowd was slowly gathering beneath the box where Gus screamed down at them, hawking and waving the roll of tickets.

Norma moved on. She stopped before the motordrome and the sign: *He Rides The Wall of Death.*

"Hi, there." A tall broad shouldered young man with curly hair was sitting side-saddle on a motorcycle on the bally platform in front of the big wooden barrel. He was smiling. "Saw you at breakfast, must be new."

"Yes," Norma said. "I'm going to dance."

"Good. They need somebody." He jumped down from the motorcycle and strode across the platform, a dashing slim hipped figure in his white breeches and calf-tight black boots, a scarlet kerchief at the throat of his open-necked white shirt. He dropped off the platform in front of her. "I'm Speed Lamston. I push the wheel in the bucket there. How about a coke?"

"I'd like it." She fell in beside him and they walked towards the lunch concession.

"Worked the carny before?"

"No, I've never even danced before."

"Gee, it must be pretty exciting for you," Speed said.

"Yes." Norma put a hand to her throat, "I'm filled up to here with it."

"I still get like that." His keen boyish face lit. "I love it. I'm just a show-off kid, I guess. If I wasn't here I'd still be running my wheel up and down the sidewalks."

They took two stools at the concession. A tired-eyed girl brought them their cokes.

"Been with the show long?" Norma asked.

"This is my first season with Kirkland. I spent two years with the Holly Burke Shows. That was a bigger show, but this was a chance to take over the drome on a percentage, and run it myself. I figure another season with Ed and maybe I can rustle up the nut to throw together my own unit. I'm already working on the silo. I got a small shack down in Florida where I winter, and I'm building the thing myself in the back yard."

"Where in Florida?"

"Just outside Sarasota. It's cheap, and it's loaded with show people."

Norma regarded Speed with new interest. He was young, below thirty, and being a daredevil you would expect him to have his head in the clouds and just not give a damn. But he wasn't like that at all.

"Ever been to Florida?" he asked her.

"No, but I've always wanted to go. I don't like the cold weather. Being in a warm climate is a kind of dream with me."

"Me too. All I remember about cold is not having enough clothes to keep me warm and my old man screaming about the heating bill."

Norma laughed, "It always killed me to see pictures of people laughing in the snow," she said. "I used to think, sure you can laugh, but you ought to try it in a cotton dress."

Speed patted her hand. It was a friendly gesture, but her heart quickened, "I guess we come from the same side of the tracks." he said, "So here's to the sunny places, but I sure wish it was a little cooler today." He drained his coke bottle, "I gotta get back. Old Wendall is over there to begin the bally, and I gotta make like a daredevil."

Norma walked along with him, enjoying just being near him. At the motordrome she met Wendell Goodwin, a fat gimlet eyed man with a leather voice. Wendell was outside talker for the girl show and did a stint for Speed as a favor. She went up the steps and stood on the platform that ran around the outside of the big wooden barrel, and watched the bally begin.

"H'yar, h'yar," Wendell bellowed. "Step right up here and see the handsome, athletic, death defying Speed Lamston defy the laws of gravity, and ride the motorcycle on the perpendicular wall."

Speed had one of the motorcycles on a set of rollers on the platform. He kicked it over until it popped and roared, the wheels spinning on the rollers.

"Don't get in front of that thing, lady," Wendell warned. "It just might take off."

The fat woman with the hotdog stuck in her face and a cotton print dress draped like a sack on the shapeless body, scurried to one side.

"H'yar, looka here, looka here, see Speed Lamston as he stands upon the motorcycle, the wheels spinning at a mile a minute ... Up he goes ... no hands ... he guides the machine with his feet ... Looka, looka ... step up here ... one mistake and it's certain death under the turning wheels."

Speed was standing on the seat of the roaring machine, his arms outstretched. He jumped, spreading both legs. The crowd gasped, and he landed on the seat.

"That ladies and gentlemen," yelled Wendell, "This is only a small sample of what you will see on the inside. There, inside that barrel, Speed will take his machine at top speed up on the sides of the wall, fearlessly defying the laws of gravity."

People began to buy tickets and file up the stairs to take their places around the edge of the drome.

Speed gave Norma a big wink and went inside the drome through a door at the bottom. Looking down, Norma watched him pick up the mike on the inside and begin his soft-voiced explanation of what he was going to do. When he said: "And please keep your hands off the cable at the top. That cable is there to stop me in case something goes wrong and the motorcycle starts to go over the top," hands came away from the cable as though it were red hot. "Thank you," Speed said.

Straddling one of the gleaming machines in the center of the silo-like drome, he kicked over the fly-wheel, twisting the gas up until the engine screamed, roaring through the straight pipes to make more noise, setting up a bouncing reverberation that was ear-shattering to the people watching. Smiling, he adjusted his crash helmet, and eased the wheels up on the slanting portion of the drome, and gave the engine some gas as he let in the clutch. The motorcycle shot forward, tearing madly around and around at the bottom. The boards rattled, the drome shook menacingly. Norma trembled. Then, he suddenly shot straight up. A woman screamed. Speed leveled and roared around the wall of the shaking drome, No hands, around and around; no feet, the boards crashing like thunder, the heavy wire guys straining, the audience silent, leaning back afraid as the wheels roared up to the wire and dipped away, dropped to the bottom and roared up again.

Afterwards, her ears still ringing, Norma saw Speed stoop out from the small doorway.

"How'd you like it?" he asked.

"I was scared stiff," Norma said, "How do *you* do it?"

He laughed, "You know, I think I like you. Let's hit the town for a couple of beers when we shut down tonight."

"I'd love to," Norma said, hoping that the eagerness was not too apparent in her voice.

"Good. It's a date."

CHAPTER SEVEN

It wasn't yet dark, but the pale gray sky was filling out with stars and the moon was already full and strangely cold and it hovered in the mid-sky.

"Benny, yer it."

"Aghhh."

"You are, yer it."

High-pitched kid voices from patches of tall grass and from behind trailers and from behind hanging sheets, white-flapping in the almost breeze.

"C'mon, c'mon. Yer it, yer it."

"I ain't."

"C'mon, Benny, ya gonna play or not?"

"Balls to you. I ain't it."

Dusk descended, softly covering. Yellow square—the lighted windows of the trailers. The milky way, now a dazzling spray across the sky; a shooting star, brightly living shortly. Unseen voices, tired now from play, irate little girl, "Gahdamn you, Benny, get offa me. Stop rassling. You know what yer Ma said. Benny! Darn you! I'm tellin'. Ma! Ma! Benny's bouncing on me!"

Norma sat in a folding chair outside the trailer, listening to the dulled night sounds, listening to the concerted croak and squall from the poultry building, the plaintive lowing of the cows. She watched the lights of the carnival beyond the wall of canvas, listened to the screams of the girls on the whirring, turning ferris wheel, the blare of the loudspeakers, the music of the hoarse-voiced talkers, the catcalls of the mothers in the trailer doorways, getting their kids in for supper before they went back to their booths.

She lifted herself from the chair and walked slowly across the field. Ducking through the canvas, she came out on the midway and went to the bally platform of the Girl Show where Wendell was making his grind. Darla and another girl were standing on the platform, draped in their faded satin capes. Both looked listless and disinterested, the gum working in their mouths, their expressions bored. Wendell was doing his best, trying to tell the growing crowd of men that the girls would be transformed into nymphs on the inside, but it was too much of a selling job.

Norma saw Lee Harker leaning against a pole at the entrance and she went over to him.

"Hiya, kid, come to see these frogs work?"

Norma did not like the expression, but she said, "I thought I might learn something."

"You'll never learn anything good from these dawgs." He jerked his head towards the platform. "Look at them. Meat. Just meat. Poor old Wendell, trying to turn a tip with those slobs for the gaff. Ugh."

"They must be tired. They've already done several shows."

"Pigs are pigs," Lee said. "Come on in." He rolled away from the pole and took her arm, guiding her through the entrance. She didn't resist his grasp. There was something about him, something commanding that made her fall in with what he suggested as though it was natural for her to do his bidding. They crossed the empty tent and went to the music stand, a low platform below the stage that was roped off from the crowd. Two men were sitting there on folded chairs, one of them smoking, his stare vacant; the other was buried in the green pages of the racing form.

"Harry," Lee said. The staring one focused his eyes. "This is Norma Chiari. She's gonna be dancing with the show. Harry Turner, he plays the clarinet and sax. Chuck Barnes." The other man was looking, mouth agape. "He blows the horn. We're all stuck with this freak show for the summer."

The customers were filing in. They moved up to the platform and stood around, waiting, shifting uncomfortably as though they were doing something wrong and might be caught at it. When a sizable group had gathered around the stage, Lee took his seat behind the drums and flexed the sticks in his hands.

"You can stand over there," he told Norma, pointing with one of the sticks. "You won't see much except a lot of shaking flesh, but you'll see it better."

The lights were glaring over the stage and Norma was glad to move into the shadows to one side. Wendell came up next to the combo and took the portable mike in his hand. The snare gave him a thrill, and he said, "Welcome to the Fabulous Follies, and now, no more waiting." He put a leer in his voice. "I know what you gentlemen are here to see and we got it … yessir … and now straight from an engagement in New Orleans, the belle of the deep south, the gor-juss Lolly Lane!"

The bass drum thumped and the muted horn took up the first bars of a swaying melody. The canvas at the end of the ramp parted and Lolly Lane appeared, smiling, arms up, a gauzy skirt hanging from her thin hips, her ribs showing, a satin bra covering her small breasts. She swiveled down the ramp and marched around the stage, shaking her shoulders. On the second turn she removed the bra to show the thin flabby breasts jouncing free, the rhine-stones covering the nipples winking in the bright light. The act was dull and apathetic and drew mild applause. Darla was next. She had more to shake and she made it suggestive coming close to the edge and letting the men grab at her big swinging breasts. She drew hoots and hollers, and a thunder of applause. The next girl was a contortionist who took everything off and stirred the imaginations with her bumps and grinds while doing a backbend. The fourth girl did a suggestive erotic number with a fur neck-piece.

When it was over and the crowd had left, Lee leaned back in his chair and said, "Learn anything?"

"Well, I...I..." Norma was still red-faced after the dance with the fur-piece.

"Nothing," Lee said. He got up and came over to her. "You know, kid, I think you've got the stuff to make a really great dancer."

She wondered why Della and this big fascinating man didn't like each other. Lee was kind, and he wanted to help her, so did Della. She would have to be very careful. She remembered the familiarity with which Lee had greeted Della. She laughed silently, the way they scrapped with each other was like they were married, except that you could sense Lee wasn't the marrying type. Besides, Della had her Gus.

She thought of Speed. There was one handsome boy. The picture of his laughing eyes and clean cut face came before her eyes as if she was looking at a movie. This was a man she could love. A warmth began to flow inside her. It rose to her breasts. Little needles of pain tingled at the tips. She touched herself in sudden clutching anxiety. That filthy truck driver. Supposing he had... She began to count on her fingers. No, she decided, it would be OK.

Norma sighed. The pain had turned to a pleasant womanly feeling. Now she was conscious of a warmth at the bottom of her tummy. Something was throbbing. She had the sensation of wanting to be comforted. So this was what thinking of Speed did to her. It was as if she had grown up all of a sudden, changing from a scared girl to a woman, with a woman's desires. Just then it seemed to present no problem, because her body was filling with pleasurable sensation.

It was difficult all at once to bring her mind back to reality.

"That bit you did this morning was terrific. Had a lot of passion in it. Tell you what. You come back here after the last show and we'll work some more. I've been thinking about this and I've got some good ideas. I'm telling you, about an hour each night, and by the end of the week you'll have an act that will knock 'em dead."

Norma felt a constriction in her chest. It had something to do with the way he was looking at her, and she felt nervous in his presence, but more than that, it was the thought of being a good dancer, better than the ordinary stripper that was overwhelming to her. Suddenly, more than anything else, she wanted that.

"What time?" she asked.

"We fold it about midnight. Come in around then. I'll have them leave the lights on."

"Thanks, Lee, I'll be here." She moved away.

"By the way, kid," Lee said, stopping her with his hand on her arm. "Don't mention this to Della, huh?" He winked. "She, uh, she might object."

Norma smiled. Della would have a fit. But Norma knew that Lee could teach her more about dancing than Della could, and she was eager to learn. Della didn't like Lee, but he seemed more than kind. "I won't say anything," she said.

"Good." He patted her arm. "See you then."

Norma went back to the trailer where she absorbed herself in Darla's copy of *Confidential* magazine. She made coffee on the small stove and then sat at the table, sipping it and reading, but unable to concentrate.

So much was happening too fast. How long ago had it been. Just two days since she had been in that shed. Two nights since the truck driver had ... what was his name? She frowned. Was it possible to forget his name? Just two nights and everything was so different. She shivered despite the heat. It was almost frightening. Was it all moving too quickly? Suddenly she was thinking about being a dancer, and there was Lee and Della and Speed. Her hand flew to her mouth. "Gosh," she said. Speed. I'll have to tell him.

Sliding off the bench, she leaped from the trailer and started across the field. She entered the midway and went to the

Motordrome. Speed was sitting on the edge of the platform and he smiled when he saw her.

"Hey, you're early. You don't want to act too eager, you know, I'm liable to get ideas."

"Speed," Norma said, "I'm awfully sorry, but I won't be able to make it tonight."

"Oh?" His voice was filled with disappointment and the smile left his face.

"I forgot that I had something to do."

"Can't it wait? I was figuring on spending the evening talking about my future, and then maybe convince you that Florida is the place for you." He was smiling and kidding, but behind it there was a serious note.

"I can't," she said. "I … I promised Della that I'd take a dancing lesson tonight."

"I'll come watch."

"No," she answered sharply. "I mean, I'd be too nervous if someone was watching. It's going to be hard enough as it is."

"Okay, I wouldn't want to make you nervous." He had regained his wide smile. "Another time."

"Please, I really want to hear all about Florida." She smiled at him as winsomely as she knew how.

"Great."

"I'm awful sorry, Speed. I just didn't think."

"Forget it, kid. I know how it is."

Wendell approached them, wheezing, mopping the sweat from his face and jowls. "Wanta work up another tip, kid?"

"Might as well," Speed jumped to his feet. "Remember, think about Florida," he said to Norma.

Turning away, Norma walked along the midway. Why had she lied to him about Della? She shrugged. It's just that it would have been harder to explain that it was Lee who was going to give her the lessons. Why she felt she would have to explain to Speed, whom she hardly knew, she did not know. But she did know that she wanted Speed to like her. He represented something to her that she liked. He was planning for the future, and he was the first man she had ever met who even thought of the future.

Inside the trailer she stretched out on the sofa and read the magazine until it was almost midnight and time to leave. She tossed the magazine aside and got up. Then she left and walked to the tent. Lee was waiting.

He was trying something on the tom-toms when she entered and he did not hear her. He was bent low over the drums and seemed to be lost, beating away slowly and softly, his head cocked to one side.

Norma listened a moment, then she moved forward. She was standing next to him before he saw her.

"I'm here," she said.

"Ahhhh. Hi. I was just fooling around here with something." He leaned back, smiling. "Have a seat. I want to explain to you first what I have in mind."

Norma stepped over the rope and took the trumpet player's chair. She sat and crossed her legs.

"Now here's the deal," Lee said. "This prancing around the stage and posing and taking off a piece of rag here and a piece there is lot a nonsense. Any stupid broad can do that. You're gonna be different. I been working this whole thing out in my mind and it sounds good. You do your act without spotlights, but we have a fire there in the middle of the stage and you dance around that. We bill you as Tamara, the Fire Goddess. Sounds corny, but it'll go great. I'll get you the costume and the props and we do the thing with drums, nothing else. You like?"

"I don't know, I guess so."

"Okay, let's get to work."

"Lee, why are you going to all this trouble?"

Lee had gotten to his feet. He hesitated, then turned and looked at her. "Partly for kicks," he said. "I take a girl who hardly knows one foot from the other and in a week I have the marks

falling over themselves to see her dance. For me that's kicks—
helping people." His eyes glowed suddenly. "And you're a damn
good-looking female. I like being around a good-looking piece of
woman. Now let's get to work!"

Norma climbed to the stage and went to the end of the
ramp. Lee came up with her and walked her through some of the
motions he wanted in the dance.

"It has to look savage. This is purely sexual, like a fertility
rite, your mind has to get across that it is the real thing. Forget
that there is an audience out there. You won't see them, once you
start dancing, you won't even hear them breathing. Just listen to
the drums, nothing else, just the drums.'"

He went back to his drums, and sat down. He started the
deep tom-tom beat, calling out the directions. Norma followed
his orders, making mistakes, but gradually getting the feel of it,
and letting the drums carry her, until she was swept up in the
rhythm, her body swaying and jerking as Lee manipulated her
with his change of beat.

They worked for an hour and Lee called a stop. "That'll do
for tonight."

Norma was breathing heavily. Her blouse was stained with
perspiration, as she came to the edge of the platform and sat
down.

"Tired?"

"Dead," she said, stretching.

"Takes a little while to get used to it. You've got it, kid." He
laughed lightly. "Wait until Kirkland catches your act. He'll flip."

"I hope you're right."

His drums were covered. "I know I'm right. Come on, I'll
walk you back to the trailer."

Norma slipped to the ground. "I think I could sleep for a
week." She wrapped her arms tightly about herself to still the odd
tingling sensation she still felt after the haunting influence of the
drums and the dancing.

There was a movement at the rear of the tent. Norma's eyes snapped up. Lee was behind the stage turning off the lights. Barnes, the man Della had told off the night before, stepped into the light from the shadows. He had been in the rear watching her dance. He ducked through the canvas flap at the opening and was gone. The lights went out, but there was still enough light filtering from the midway to see inside the tent. Lee came to her side and took her arm.

"That man, Barnes, was in the back watching," Norma said. "He just ran out."

"Oh, yeah. He probably went to start your first fan club." Lee laughed, but Norma felt a strange sensation, a feeling of foreboding.

They stepped into the midway and started across. Norma glanced to the right towards the concession and Speed was sitting at the counter, a cup of coffee at his elbow. He saw her come out of the tent, and Norma winced as she saw his expression harden. He turned back to his coffee.

Caught in her small lie, and seeking to rationalize it in her own mind, Norma resorted to anger. What has he got to be mad about. I don't owe him anything. I don't even know him. Despite this, she knew that she was in the wrong, that Speed did mean something to her even if she had only met him that day, or rather that she wanted him to mean something to her and now it was spoiled. Lee's hand was around her upper arm and she pressed it to her side. His fingers touched her breast, but she kept the pressure there.

They crossed the silent field without speaking. The trailer was dark. Lee had not spoken since they left the tent. At the trailer he stopped, still holding her arm, and turned her.

She smiled at him gratefully.

"Lee, I want to thank you for ..."

He silenced her with a finger over her lips. He tilted her chin and his face hovered over hers. Her heart was beating faster. She saw his big face come down until it was a blur. His lips touched hers lightly and he pulled her to him until she was outlined against him. She trembled, feeling the excitement growing within her. She sensed his own increasing passion and strangely enough was not afraid. She closed her eyes and held her breath. He kissed her hard and her senses reeled.

Then she realized she was shaking, "I better go in," she said, her voice strangely hoarse. Lee said nothing, smiling he released her arms. She turned quickly and pulled open the trailer door. She stepped inside and closed the door, leaning back against it, breathing hard and feeling frightened. Her whole body was trembling. She bit down on her lower lip and pushed away from the door.

Then she realized she was shaking, and pushed him away. "I better go in," she said, her voice strangely hoarse. Lee said nothing. Smiling, he released her arms. She turned quickly and pulled open the trailer door. She stepped inside and closed the door, leaning back against it, breathing hard and feeling frightened. Her whole body was trembling. She bit down on her lower lip and pushed away from the door.

Moonlight slanted through the small windows. The sofa bed was not in use, so Darla was no doubt out on the town. Without turning on the lights, she went through the trailer to the large bed, unbuttoning the blouse as she moved. She pulled the blouse off and put it aside. She kicked off her shoes, then unzipped the slacks and slipped them off, putting them with the blouse. She removed the rest of her clothes and stretched, the moonlight bathing her nudity. She pulled back the bed sheet and stiffened. Behind her the door clicked. Her fingers tightened on the sheet and her heart thumped. The door opened.

"Darla?" she whispered.

The scrape of footsteps and the door closed. A scream gathered in her throat. "Darla?"

"It's me."

"Lee! But, ... Lee, I'm ... I mean I'm going to bed."

"Norma." There was a strange inflection in his voice, an aching sound. His shadowy figure moved towards her.

Norma cowered, her breathing stopped. She shook her head from side to side. "Lee, no," she whispered. "Lee, please ... I ... "

He stood over her. The moonlight crossed his face. Looking up, she saw the longing in his eyes, the wanting that was etched in his expression. The years of being unloved and unwanted came back to her with a rush, the years of growing up when she was just another mouth to be fed, another body to be clothed. He wanted her. She gasped and threw herself forward, clinging. "Lee, Lee ... please," she whispered.

His arms encircled her, pressed her close. Her face was hard against his chest. She savored the man-sweat of him. He gripped her arms and eased her back until her legs touched the edge of the bed. He pressed her down and she relaxed. Her shoulders touched bed and he hovered over her. He brought his head down and kissed the hollows of her neck. Norma lay motionless, thrilling as his lips moved lightly over her. She felt her breasts swelling. Her breath came in tiny gasps. Tenderly, he kissed one breast, then the other. They were hard and aching. "Lee, no please." Norma took a deep breath. She flung her head back, closing her eyes. His hands and lips left her. She opened her eyes, wondering what had happened.

She saw him then, standing over her. She watched his fingers move with deliberate calm over the buttons of his shirt. He shrugged the shirt away and it dropped at his feet. Not for a moment did he take his eyes away from her. His burning gaze increased her unwilling ardor. Her nerves seemed to be screaming. He tugged at his belt. His trousers dropped. He kicked them away. He pulled away his shorts and she saw him. She could not move her eyes. Remembering the terrible pain of the night before, she was rigid with fear. Slowly, he took off his shoes and socks, and stood before her, pale white in the moonlight. He was a magnificent man.

With a sharp cry she threw herself to the edge of the bed as an unbelievable passion raged through her. She grasped his arms and drew him to her and her quivering lips found him.

His breath came in sharply. A gargled cry left his throat. He grabbed her hair jerking her head back. Her hands clawed at him Roughly he threw her back on the bed. She lay moaning, then squirming, tossing in agony. Lee watched her. His mouth was quivering as he slid onto the bed next to her. She threw herself against him and drew back in sudden shuddering panic as she felt him between her thighs. His lips covered her breasts, the end of his tongue, hot and moist, sliding over them and through the deep channel between. His legs moved against hers, slowly, methodically, as his hands roamed over her; experienced hands that sought out the places that excited her most.

Norma moaned, with the ecstatic, nerve-jangling agony that enveloped her. She had no control over herself now. She wanted none, as she wallowed in the frantic passion building and building inside her until she writhed and shook under his maddening touch.

Now he was gently moving his body on top of hers, covering her and pressing down hard on her passion swollen breasts. She gasped and a tremor shook her. Their sweat mingled. He pushed himself down, sliding over her, his lips touch-her as he moved, his tongue always caressing her, bringing her to the white heat of womanly passion, till she was rolling and squirming in the anguish of fulfilment. "Lee—please," she cried.

She slammed her fists on the bed and her body jerked involuntarily, a strangled sob gagged in her throat. Her hands buried her fingers in his hair, holding him to her as she arched her back. Unintelligible sounds were gushing from her throat, closing her eyes against the spinning, exploding flashes.

She pulled his head away and dragged his heavy body up over her. His mouth covered hers. Her lips met his hot tongue. She took her hands from his head and slipped them down and under him and found him and brought him to her. Scarcely knowing what she was doing, she held him at the edge until she found the place, then she lunged up against him, and screamed with the sudden delicious pain. She could think of nothing, as her body wildly sought deliverance from the longing.

"Lee, please." Her voice was rising and falling. She dug her hands into his hard back, as the rapture spread all over her. How strong he was! He seemed to be filling her whole body. All her ragged, jangling nerve endings had converged on one place in her. Now she had no will of her own. She was suspended in space. The wild agony shook her. Something wondrous was happening inside of her. She was being flung through space. From far away she heard his voice.

"Now, baby, now! Come on!" Lee's gasping, hard-breathing voice filled the warm darkness.

"Now, now, now!" Wildly lunging, convulsing, light-spinning, exploding.

Then quiet as the explosive door to peace burst inside her.

CHAPTER EIGHT

Norma awoke slowly. She twisted in the tangle of sheets and stretched. She felt blissfully calm and lazy. She opened her eyes and the sun was streaming in through the windows. She turned and looked for Darla. The sofa bed was closed and the trailer was silent. Outside were the sounds of morning. She burrowed back into the bed, not wanting to move.

Her feelings about the previous night were a mixture of guilt and wonderful pleasure. She remembered everything in vivid detail, and in so remembering, one thing struck her as strange and nagged at her with a vague annoyance. She had never experienced anything quite like it, but she now recalled that she had been the one who had forced the actual act of love-making, and she remembered Lee's calm approach, the way he had carefully brought her to the point of agony. In a sense, he had turned her on as if she were some sort of machine, and this made her uneasy.

Rising from the bed, she showered and then dressed, then she stood before the mirror and combed her hair. She wondered what she would say when she saw Lee. It frightened her a little. What did he feel? Had she been just another easy conquest for him? She shuddered at the thought. He had wanted her, she had seen it in his face. But was he in love with her? The comb stopped and she stared hard at her image in the glass. Was she in love with him? This had not yet crossed her mind, and now it baffled her. Was this then what love was? A terrible animal longing? She had always supposed that she would know the man she loved before she slept with him, and somehow it had always been involved with marriage. But last night she had never thought of love or marriage, she just wanted the man. She frowned, not understanding. She had behaved like an animal.

The clock told her that it was too late for breakfast. She left the trailer to look for Della.

The sky was stark and hot except for a foreboding dark streak that hovered along the northwest horizon. Ed Kirkland was standing in the field, his hands on his hips, staring at the distant suggestion of bad weather. When he saw Norma he waved. Then he walked towards her with the lumbering gait of the fat man.

"Howdy, there, kid."

"Hello, Mr. Kirkland."

Norma stopped and shaded her eyes against the sun. Kirkland had a straw tilted over his forehead.

"Howya like the carny life?"

"It's just wonderful."

"How are the dancing lessons?"

Norma startled. What did he mean by that? Has Lee ...? She trembled slightly, frightened, then gathered herself together. It was only natural that he should ask. He had hired her as a dancer. She suddenly realized she felt more guilt than she had imagined. "They're okay," she said.

"Good. How about those scratches, they healing?"

"Yes. I don't even notice them now."

He smiled warmly. "This ain't a bad life, Norma. I been at it for a lot of years and I ain't never tired of it. If you really get the sawdust in your shoes and you treat the carny right, it'll treat you good right back."

Norma did not answer, and no answer was expected. Kirkland was merely telling her that there was a place for her with his show. He began to walk towards the midway and she fell in beside him.

"Folks say a lot of bad things about the carny life," he continued. "You hear about it being crooked and dirty and that the people are immoral." He snorted derisively. "Pure crap. You find some bad ones, just like you do in any business. We got drunks, but hell, there's drunks everywhere. We got whores too, but it's always the *respectable* gentlemen with the price to pay that makes them whores. For the most part you'll find that carny folks are as good citizens as the next. They marry and raise kids and pay their taxes just like anybody else. I ain't saying we're angels. Hell, we fall on our prat as much as anybody when it comes to toeing the line. But I will say that if a person wants to live a clean, moral life, he can do it as well with a carnival as any place else."

Norma narrowed her eyes. Was he just talking in a general way, or was he really trying to tell her something? Did he know about last night? It wasn't possible. Not unless Lee... Oh, my God, could he ...? She was seized with a sudden terror. Then she saw Della standing by the lunch concession.

"There's Della," she said. "Mr. Kirkland, I have to see her."

"Go ahead. See you around, kid."

She moved away with long strides. The grass on the midway was trampled flat. The clean-up crew was busy collecting the refuse that was all that was left of last night's crowd. The rakes stirred up dust and the men shuffled through it.

"Hey, Norma."

Norma turned and stopped. Speed Lamston stood by one of his motorcycles, a wrench in one hand and a grease rag in the other. He was wearing soiled coveralls. "Wait a minute," he called. He put the wrench down and came across the platform, wiping his hands. He jumped to the ground. "Ain'ja talking to me?"

"I didn't see you, I was ..."

He grinned, still wiping his hands. He paused and ran one hand through his tousled blonde hair, leaving a streak of grease. Instinctively, Norma's hand went up towards his hair, but she stopped.

"You have grease in your hair now," she said.

"I'll be covered before I'm done," he said. "One of my vices. I get near grease, I get covered. Paint anything, I get more paint on me."

"You need a wife to take care of you." It was a simple statement, the kind you might make as a retort to what he had said, actually a joke; but Speed sobered.

"You're right," he said softly. Norma paused, not knowing what to answer and there was a gap of silence.

"Say," he said, "about last night. I, uh...I mean when you came out of the tent and I gave you a hard look, well, I..."

"Speed, I'm sorry," Norma blurted. "I really am." She dropped her eyes. "I...I don't know why I lied to you about Della, but I..." She couldn't find the right words. "It's just that I want to learn so badly. I..."

He touched her arm. "Look, Norma. If anything, I'm flattered that you bothered to lie to me. Hell, you don't owe me anything. If I gotta convince you to go out with me, okay. I figure if you see something you like then you ought to be glad to..."

Norma choked suddenly and tears welled in her eyes. It would have been easier if he were angry. She turned and suddenly ran.

"Hey..."

She didn't listen. She ran to the concession. Della was gone. Gus was sitting at the counter, a wry smile twisting his freckled, simian face.

"Where's Della?"

"She went over to the tent to do some work on her act," Gus said. Norma started away, but he came off the stool and took her arm, detaining her. "Wait a minute, kid."

"What?"

Still holding her arm, he walked away from the concession. "Della's a little miffed," he said shyly. "I think you oughta let her cool off a bit before you talk to her."

"What's wrong?"

"Nothing much, kid. She's just a little hurt, that's all. Sam Barnes has been mouthing around some talk about you and Lee Harker being together last night."

"What!?"

"Now don't in a uproar," Gus said, placating her. "Nobody takes what Barnes says very seriously. He said that you were taking lessons from Lee last night. He just didn't say what kind of lessons."

Norma felt a constriction in her chest and she thought for a moment that she was going to be sick. "Oh, Gus, why do people have to be so cruel about things."

"Now, now, kid, take it easy." He patted her arm. He rummaged in his shirt pocket and brought out a crumpled pack of cigarettes. "Here, have a smoke."

Norma took the cigarette and when she held it for Gus' match, her hand was shaking. She gulped the smoke and coughed. They had walked past the entrance arch and were crossing the sunhard grass. Gus stopped and looked back.

"Della was just annoyed because she told you to stay away from Lee, and she sort of feels that she found you, and ... well, I guess it's just maternal. You see, she's got this thing about Lee. She figures he's rotten. I don't know, he might be, I just don't know. I know he's left a trail of broken hearts and busted cherries all the way from Jacksonville, but what the hell, any girl that gets tangled up with Lee certainly knows what he's after. She's either a damn fool or she's got hot pants awful bad. I don't care who the guy is, when a girl puts it on the line for him he's going to grab it."

The smoke was suddenly acrid tasting in Norma's throat. She felt foolish listening to Gus. She was trembling and near tears.

"I felt like belting Barnes," Gus said, "but he really wasn't saying anything that you could pin down as wrong. It was just the insinuation. But, like I told Della, any kid that would almost tear herself to shreds getting away from it, wasn't going to let herself get tumbled by Lee. But I guess she's just sore about you not listening to her."

"What'll I do?"

"Nothing to do. She'll get over her mad, she always does. Then she'll feel rotten about it." He chuckled. "I guess it's just that she's a female, but every time that Lee goes after a new broad, it makes her boil. Thinks of what happened to her when she was a girl, I guess." Gus started back towards the midway, "I just wanted to set you straight before you saw the others."

Norma returned to the trailer and lounged away the morning in a state of despondency. She had been a fool. She made up her mind not to make a repeat of last night. It was obvious that she didn't mean anything to Lee. It was finished. She set her mouth in hard lines. She would learn to dance. She would be better than anything they had seen. And they could all go to hell!

By afternoon it was too hot to stay in the trailer. She went outside and walked to a cluster of trees that offered some shade and a soft, green blanket of grass. For an hour she practiced exercises that Lee had explained would help her, then she went to the trailer and showered, and then to the midway where the crowds were growing.

She went to the Ten-in-one where a show was in progress. The crowd, led by Gus with his mike, was now standing before the small proscenium where Della sat at her table surrounded by the red velvet curtain. Della was dressed in a robe of flowing white, with astrological symbols embroidered on the hem. Her blonde hair cascaded down her back and a band of gilt leather studded with glass jewels was around her forehead. She was unsmiling and her eyes flashed.

"Now, then, folks, I call your attention to madam Della,—who has in her care the mysteries and secrets of the past—she sees all and knows all—she tells you your most inner-most secret—she sees the present the past and the future. Now I am going to pass among you and hand out these cards and envelopes. If you want to ask Madam Della a question you write it on the card and seal it in the envelope. Here you are m'am. You too, sir. Please sign your initials or your name."

Norma stood at the edge of the group. She knew that Della had seen her, but she made no sign. Gus collected the sealed envelopes and took them to the stage. Della reached down for them and then placed the small stack on the table before her. She came to her feet and held up the first envelope. She tilted her head back, as though summoning help from the air. Her eyes were closed and she held the white envelope high away from her. Her lips moved soundlessly.

Norma glanced at the crowd and smiled. They were already entranced. The handfuls of popcorn were poised between the bag and the gaping mouths. They stared at the woman in white who was doing her act. It was the *one-ahead,* as Della had explained it in the truck the first night. Norma looked around and picked out the "stick" in the audience. It was the wife of one of the flat-joint operators who did odd jobs around the midway when she wasn't helping her husband. Della would simply make up any initials and make up the answer to a non-existent question and the "stick" would agree that it was correct. Then Della opened the envelope and she was ready with the next question.

Della lowered her arm and slowly opened her eyes. "I have an initial," she said, her voice lower and huskier than usual. "I have the initial N." She paused. "And I have the initial C. N.C." She stared over the heads of the people, looking at none of them. "This is a young girl. She is far from home and she is alone. She is troubled." Her voice was as steady as the tolling of a bell "You have friends, N.C., but you must trust them and abide by their counsel. They are older and wiser than you and they know what they're talking about. You do not believe this because you are young and your heart is easily turned, but you must take care for disaster is lurking in the shadows." She closed her eyes and her voice rose. "This man is not for you. He thinks only of lust. He would use you and cast you aside."

A sharp cry left Norma's throat. She clapped a hand to her mouth. The heads snapped around, the staring, quizzical eyes falling on her. With a sharp intake of breath, Norma whirled and ran from the tent.

A tiny smile crossed Della's face as she tore open the envelope.

CHAPTER NINE

"Hyah, hyah, step right up here, ladies and gentlemen! See the finest show in the midway! Looka here! Looka here! Yes, yes, yes. Step right up here! She shimmies, she shakes, she shows you the delectable sights of the female form. You ain't seen nothin' like this since they closed the burly-Q in Kansas City. Hyar, hyar, get up close here and get your tickets. For the small price of one half dollar you can walk right inside that tent and see what those lovely young ladies have in store for you. Yessir! Less than the price of a movie. I can't tell you what they do because there are ladies present, but oh, my! Sorry, sonny, you wouldn't know what they were doing if I let you in."

Wendall was grinding, his voice like a file running over metal, a chest-deep bellow over the portable loudspeaker. The sweat ran over his face and into the creases of his jowls and over his stained and wilted collar. The Saturday night crowd pressed up to his box, their vacant faces waiting and expecting. The music wailed, and the sound of the crowd was a discordant hum that rose and fell and was punctuated by laughter and squeals and screams and the leather-voiced chant of the hawkers.

"Hurry, hurry, hurry! You ain't been to the Fair until you been to this show. You'll see shimmering beauty displayed the way nature made it. And tonight, and only tonight, you will see the daring fire dance! From the jungles of the Amazon comes Tamara, the Fire Goddess, to do her daring dance of the flames!"

In the dressing tent, Norma paced back and forth. She could hear Wendall only faintly. She had butterflies in her stomach!

Her nervousness made the palms of her hands sweat. She rubbed her hands together.

"Sit down," Darla snapped, "you're even making me nervous." She was adjusting the rhinestones to her breasts.

Norma kept walking, the faded cotton wrapper that covered her, swished about her bare legs. Now she wished that she hadn't been so eager to make up her body. She could certainly use something to do. She stopped and looked into the mirror. Her hair fell straight down her back, and the heavy, exaggerated make-up on her face made her look like a stranger to herself. She went to one of the folding chairs and sat down.

"Take it easy, kid," Lolly Lane said, shifting her gum. "You show that bunch of jerks them tits of yours, they're gonna go nuts. You could just go out there and sit on a box and you'd have 'em flippin'."

The clarinet player stuck his head into the dressing tent. "Hey, couple you broads make the bally, huh?"

"That's me, I guess," Darla said, "Come on, Lolly."

"How about her?" Lolly said, jerking her finger at Norma. "Don't she have to make a bally?"

"No," Darla said flatly.

"Why not? Cripes, what's she, a star or something? Hell just because she's got those big nuts on her you'd think…"

"Shut up, and come on," Darla said, "Kirkland says she's just gonna dance."

Lolly went up the steps to the ramp, but she stopped at the canvas and said, "Pure crap, I say." There was venom in her voice. "I knew she was humping it with Lee, and now Kirkland. Holy mackerel, I didn't even know he could get it up."

Norma's eyes blazed and she came storming off the chair, but the girl was gone.

"Don't panic, kid," the girl with the fur neckpiece said. "Lolly gets a little bitchy about this time of the month."

Slumping down in the chair, Norma worried her hands, wondering if she was going to be able to dance. She had worked hard for a week. Every night she came to the tent and met Lee and practiced under his instructions. And then ... she didn't want to think about it. She had made up her mind that Lee wasn't going to have her again, but the minute his hands touched her she was gone, and there nothing she could do to stop herself. Then Darla had come into the trailer and seen them making love and now it was common knowledge that Lee was her lover. There was a casual acceptance among the carny people, but Norma could not get used to it. She was assailed with a deep-set feeling of guilt. Every day she swore that it was not going to happen again, and then it was night and Lee was there, big, naked, demanding....

"Hi!"

Norma glanced up towards the opening in the rear of the tent. Speed Lamston had his head stuck inside.

"Pay your half-a-buck and get your kicks on the outside, boy," one of the girls said.

"I come bearing gifts." He stepped inside and he held a large, flat box under his arm. He crossed to Norma and handed it to her. "For your opening night," he said, placing the box in her lap.

Norma stared at it, not daring to touch it. She swallowed hard, unable to speak. It was the first time she had ever been given a gift.

"Open it," Speed said. The other two girls had gathered around.

"What is it?" Norma asked apprehensively.

"Open it and see," Speed said, his face beaming.

"For heaven's sake, open the box before I bust a blood vessel," one of the girls said.

"Hey! Whatcha got?" Darla appeared at the top of the ramp with Lolly behind her, the bally completed.

Norma lifted the lid of the box and pulled aside the tissue paper to reveal the white terrycloth robe. "A robe," she breathed. Darla whistled.

Anxious to please her, Speed took the box from her and lifted the robe from it, shaking it out. "Come on, try it on."

Delighted with the gift, Norma leaped to her feet and shrugged out of the cotton wrapper. Except for a grass kirt that hung low on her full hips and reached her ankles, she was naked. Her body had been darkened with makeup and it glistened with oil. The nipples of her breasts had been daubed with rouge. Speed stiffened and his breath came in sharply. His arms shot out, holding the robe, as though to cover her from his own eyes. Norma slid her arms into the full sleeve and pulled the robe about her. She whirled, hugging it close to her throat.

"Oh, it feels so good!" Beside herself, she threw herself on Speed's chest and hugged him. "Oh, Speed, thank you!"

"She must be working the whole damn show, Lolly said from the side of her mouth.

Norma whirled. "Now wait just a minute, you!"

Wendall's voice interrupted the threatened outbreak. He was talking on the inside mike. "And now gentlemen, without further adoo, the Fab-u-luss Follies will get underway. I know what you're here to see and we got more than enough." He chuckled and the crowd beyond the canvas laughed.

"You're on, Lolly," Darla said.

Lolly tossed her hair and walked to the steps. She climbed them without looking back. She stood there a moment, then the music began. She hefted her breasts in her hands, parted the canvas with an elbow, and stepped through.

"I gotta get back to the drome," Speed said.

"Speed, I just don't know what to say. This was such a nice surprise."

"That's saying plenty," he said. "I gotta get. Good luck tonight, honey." He turned quickly and dashed through the opening in the tent. Norma stared for a long moment at the moving canvas.

"That's a nice guy," Darla said.

"Yes." There was a wistful tinge to her voice and a pang of sadness came over her.

"I think if he gave me a tumble I could give up hustling," Darla said. "He's a lotta man."

Norma turned away and went back to the chair and sat down. She fingered the nap of the robe. If only she hadn't met Lee. If only Speed were the only one.

Rippling applause, and Lolly appeared. She stomped down the steps, her high heels clattering. She held her G-string and bits of gauze in her hands. "Rough bastards out there this trip," she said. "I hadda peel down to the skin to get anything outta them."

"Maybe they like 'em plump," Darla said as she mounted the stairs and stood waiting. She took her cue and flashed a lot of teeth and went through the canvas.

Norma closed her eyes and tried to relax. She could hear the audience reacting to Darla's act, and the sound of it was frightening. It was the sound of a monster, a humming, predatory beast that she must placate.

"They oughta have an annex here," the contortionist said.

"Yeah, but Kirkland don't like it."

"That's stupid. We could make a mint in this town. I was out with a deputy last night and he says they let everything go if it's quiet."

"Kirkland says, no annex."

"I can't see the difference. Hell, that's the best part of my act," the contortionist said.

"What's an annex?" Norma asked.

"Boy, you really are a greenie," Lolly said. "The annex is where you do a special show for an extra price after the regular show. You get the real hungry stags and you dirty it up. As a rule you do the annex down in the audience and all the boys cop a feel. The girls get a percentage of the annex take, but Kirkland won't allow it."

"He's a Jerk!" the contortionist said.

"With Peggy it's a matter of professional pride," Lolly said. "She does a split and picks up a silver dollar." She laughed "She left her last show because they nick-named her The Snapper."

"Aw, drop dead!" the contortionist said. Lolly doubled with laughter.

Darla returned, sweating and breathing heavily. The contortionist went on and then the girl with the fur piece.

Norma heard the beat of the tom-tom begin, a low throb. She was trembling when she got to her feet. Norma squeezed her arm.

"Just take it easy, kid," Darla said. "It's always tough until you get on the other side of the canvas."

Norma nodded. She removed the robe and folded it over the back of a chair, then she fluffed her hair, took one last look in the large mirror, and climbed the steps.

" … from deep in the jungles of the Amazon, a savage beauty who was high priestess of fire. You will see her now as she dances the sacred rites of the flame. Tamara!"

The drum beat rose and Norma felt herself being drawn to the beat. It was like a hypnotic trance. Her breathing quickened and the blood seemed to throb in her veins. She pushed aside the canvas and stepped through.

Except for the flames leaping from the brazier in the middle of the stage, the tent was dark. There was absolute silence. The wavering, flickering flames threw grotesque shadows and her body glistened in the dim light. Except for the general intake of breath and some low whistles, she was oblivious to the crowd. She gave herself to the beat of the drums. It was as though she had no will of her own, and she felt her body begin to sway. A strange excitement clutched at her loins and spread slowly up through her body. The dull throb of the drums engulfed her. She moved her feet and legs with exaggerated gestures. A hard, sharp beat on the drum and her body jerked as though some force had pulled her tendons. Her hips writhed and her arms moved with sinuosity.

Once off the ramp, she encircled the fire. As she moved past the brazier, she tossed a powder Lee had given her into the flames, and the flames leaped up. She whirled away, her hair flying wildly, her body gyrating and twisting. The sensation that had spread through her body had heightened with her movements and now she tingled. She knew what it was. It was the combination of Lee and the drums. They were inseparable to her. As he could manipulate her with his hands, he could do the same thing with the drums. And she could do nothing to stop it. She was oblivious to the audience surrounding her, the flames highlighting the gaping stares, the tongues running over lips. In the grip of the drums she felt her breasts swell with passion, the tips protruding like tiny questing fingers. Her lips pulled back from her teeth and she moaned, her hands sliding slowly up over her body until they cupped her breasts. She squeezed her aching bosoms and cried out, her body grinding and jerking. She threw her head forward and the mass of black hair spilled over her face. She flung her head back, her eyes glittering. She whirled and turned, moving around the fire as though it were her lover, coming closer and closer to the flames, feeling the heat upon her.

It was an orgiastic rite and the audience sensed it. She crouched near the flames and brought her hands slowly up her legs. Her head was back, her body arched, and the fingers moved slowly until they converged at the juncture of her thighs. There was no sound but the tom-tom and her own hard breathing. Her body shuddered and she straightened, bringing her hands up, up, over her breasts, and then up through her hair, a wanton smile on her face as she pulsated with a delicious agony.

The beat increased in tempo and she moved with it, writhing and twisting with undulating sexual movements, until it was an exploding crescendo, and with her legs spread and her body arched, she felt the muscular convulsions that brought her up on her toes as a scream tore from her throat.

The drums stopped. Her chin fell forward and she backed away from the flames, her body trembling. She slumped to the stage and her head rested on her knees.

Applause, mixed with shouts and whistles, brought her from her exhausted reverie. She looked about her, startled and frightened, then she came to her feet and ran up the ramp until she was in darkness. She parted the canvas and slipped through, standing for a moment on the small platform to collect her thoughts. The roar of the crowd was deafening. She had been a success. The girls were silent as she descended the steps and Darla lifted the robe for her to put on.

"Thanks," Norma said, breaking the silence.

"Kid, you were great!" Darla exclaimed.

"Terrific," Lolly said. "I got to admit you don't belong on no bally platform."

Norma slumped into the chair and pulled the robe tight about her. Within minutes Ed Kirkland bulled into the dressing tent, his round face beaming. "Norma, you're great!" he bellowed. He crossed to her chair and grasped Norma's hand. "If I didn't see it I wouldn't have believed it."

Della and Gus came in next. For the past week Della had been cool towards her, but now her smile on Norma was warm. "I just knew you had it, baby," she said. "What a dance!"

"The customers are still hanging on the ropes," Gus said. "There's gonna be an upsurge in rape cases tonight."

Speed was hanging in the background. He winked and held up his hand, the thumb and forefinger forming a circle. Norma smiled, stunned, but enjoying the accolades.

The dressing tent became crowded, but Lee did not appear. Norma kept looking for him, her heart pounding. More than anything, this was his triumph. She wanted him to share it, but he did not show.

Kirkland was thumping his chest. "She's the greatest attraction since 'little Egypt.' Yessir. Tomorrow we gotta get new banners painted."

"You forgetting we gotta tear down tonight? We open in Kankakee tomorrow night."

"So we open with new banners," Kirkland said.

The crowd milled around the tent until Wendall said, "You want me to start a new bally. We ought to pack 'em in for next few shows. The customers are talking all over the midway."

"You damn well bet I do," Kirkland said.

The others left the tent and only the dancers remained. "Well, kid," Darla said. "Now you're gonna grind that butt until your guts shake loose."

From beyond the wall of canvas came the stentorian bleat of Wendall's voice. "Hurry, hurry, hurry! See the daring delights! Hurry, hurry, hurry! Step up here and get your tickets while you can. See the sensational Tamara do her thrilling dance of the flames! Hurry, hurry, hurry! See the daring delights as she whirls and ..."

CHAPTER TEN

There were still people—the diehards—milling about on the midway, but the roustabouts were tearing down around them. The Carny wasted no time to fold when they had taken the last dime. There was a long night's drive ahead, and the job of setting up the moment they arrived at the next stop.

Norma was numb with exhaustion. The other girls had left the dressing tent as they completed their final act. Only she was left. She sat in the folding chair, her eyes closed, her hands still trembling; hoping that Lee would come back and say something to her. More than anything, she wanted his approval.

When Lee did not come and her breathing had returned to normal, she pulled the robe tightly about her and got to her feet. She was about to change to her clothes when one of the canvas-men put his head into the tent.

"Hurry it up, girlie. This canvas is coming down. We gotta get outta here tonight."

She decided to dress at the trailer. Taking her clothes from the nail in the upright pole, she folded them over her arm. She stooped through the flap in the tent, which put her behind the midway. Since she was covered only by the robe, she decided not to cross the midway. She started off through the tangle of parked trucks.

It was a warm night, the stillness rent only by the shouts and curses of the roughnecks as they brought the Carny to the ground. A bright, three-quarter moon shouldered the dense maze of stars.

Tired, and absorbed in her thoughts, Norma walked slowly, skirting the trucks. She was annoyed that Lee had not said anything to her during or after the shows. The last show had been jammed with customers to see her act. In one night she had become the talk of the Carnival. And it was all Lee's doing. Why had he stayed away? She also wondered about their last times together. Lee seemed distant, almost bored. It was never the same as the first night. She expected some tenderness, at least some talk of his love for her, but he was strangely silent, and the previous night he had come to the trailer; removed his clothing without speaking. He had taken her roughly, without bothering to arouse her, and then had left. She had cried slightly before falling asleep. And now he seemed to be ignoring her. It was confusing and it wounded her pride.

Without realizing it, she had left the trucks and had kept walking. She crossed the field and then she found herself in the darkness of the small stand of trees where she had practiced her exercises.

She stopped and laughed at her preoccupation, but now that she was in this pleasant spot, she sank down to the cool grass and just sat there, hugging her knees close to her. She tilted her head back, and up through the branches and leaves she could see the stars. She leaned back on her elbows and watched the sky. Everything was so peaceful. It was as though she had found a secret place that was far away from the clamor of the Carny coming down. She smiled, enjoying the sensation of being apart.

A sudden movement nearby startled her. She caught her breath and began to rise. A dark figure darted from behind a tree and pounced upon her. She opened her mouth to scream, and a hand clamped over her mouth. She struggled, her heart beating wildly, but the work-hardened body held her down and the hand over her mouth was like a band of steel. The man's face was close to hers, his fetid breath sickening her. Sam Barnes!

"Take it easy, baby," he sneered through his broken teeth. He gripped her arm with his free hand and pressed with his fingers until the pain made her gag. "Just take it easy!"

Norma stopped struggling. He released her arm. Her body was stiff with terror, and he was grinning down at her, the hand still clamped to her mouth. "I bin watchin' you. You knew I was watchin' you, didn't ya?" He chuckled. "Too bad I can't let ya answer, but I guess you'd just holler. You think I ain't good enough for ya, huh. But you're going to find out. I'm good. I am."

Norma stared with panic and loathing at the grinning face that hovered close above her.

"Oh, yeah, baby, I been watching you real close." Barnes pulled a soiled kerchief from his pocket and rolled it into a ball with one hand. Suddenly, he slammed her across the face. She gasped and he jerked his hand away. Before she could react and close her mouth, he jammed the kerchief between her teeth. She coughed, but he clamped his hand down again. Then he reached back and got another dirty kerchief. "I always carry two," he said, still grinning. "My job gets sweaty. But you won't mind, will ya?" He shook out the kerchief and took one end, laying it carefully across her chin. He then forced it under his hand that held her mouth, and the two ends dangled free on either side of her face. "Now then!"

Norma knew he was going to release her mouth and she tensed herself to struggle. But he was too fast. The hand flew away from her mouth. He gripped both ends of the kerchief and pulled down hard. She tried to wriggle free, but he held her down with his body and spread legs. Slowly, laughing lightly to himself, he forced her head to one side and tied the ends of the kerchief behind her neck. He brought both hands away and she was gagged.

"I'm strong, huh? You didn't know old Barnes was that strong, did you?"

Norma flailed at him with both hands, but he gripped her shoulders and gouged her with his thumbs. She stopped her struggle.

Lee! her mind screamed. Lee! Don't let him do this to me! I can't have this happen to me again. Lee, where are you? Oh, dear god, please! Somebody stop him!

"I'll get outta this crumby show tonight," he said. "I figured to jump it tonight, anyway. But I wasn't gonna leave until I had a crack at you. Oh, yes, baby, I been watching you doing that dance every night." He yanked aside the lapels of the robe, exposing her full rounded breasts that had become even larger and more beautiful since Lee had been loving her. His eyes shone and a trickle of saliva ran from the corner of his mouth. He licked his lips. He stared at her breasts and his mouth trembled.

Powerless under his steel-like embrace, Norma felt herself violated by his lusting eyes. She clamped her eyes closed in the vain hope that it was all a nightmare that would dissolve, but knowing that it was real, too real, feeling the man covering her like an animal.

His lips were hot and moist against her throat. She shuddered. He gripped one of her breasts and jammed his mouth on it. A wave of nausea assailed her, but Norma's mind began to click with methodical calm. She arched her back, pressing the breast to him, squirming as though she enjoyed his touch. He took his mouth away, but she moved her arms around him, pulling him to her. For an instant Barnes was surprised and wary. Then his ego asserted itself, and he believed that she wanted him. He brought his face down to nuzzle the deep valley of her bosom, relaxing with the movement. "So you like it, kid," he cried. "I thought you would."

Norma twisted suddenly. Taken by surprise, Barnes rolled over on his side. She brought her leg up and her knee slammed hard into his groin. Barnes gasped, a startled cry sagging in his throat. His hands freed her. He doubled over, a look of sick hurt on his face, clutching frantically at his belly.

Scrambling to her feet, Norma grasped the kerchief and tore it away from her bruised mouth. She spit the sodden ball of the second kerchief from her mouth. She ran, mindless of direction. Grunting with agony, Barnes lurched to his feet.

"You miserable bitch," he snarled. He came after her, running in a crouch.

Norma stopped suddenly and screamed, the sound a high-pitched wail of terror. She was running away from the trailers. She set off again, heading to the edge of the clearing, to get back closer to the trailers, but Barnes cut her off. She saw him coming and screamed again. "Help! Lee, help! Help!" The screams were lost in the sounds of the Carny, the loud bellowing of the canvas boss, the grinding of the tractor, the rasp of metal turning, the clang of wrenches, and the ringing of the mallets on iron stakes.

Barnes bulled into her. Norma fell hard, sprawling; kicking and scratching as she went down. Barnes rolled on past her and she scrambled to her knees. She screamed again. He whirled and came after her again. She was crawling as he threw himself on her, pulling her down. Then he rolled with her until he was on top of her. He slammed his hand over her mouth and she bit down hard. He cried out, tearing his hand away. She tasted blood.

He slammed his fist into the side of her face and her head seemed to explode. Her face was numb. She brought her hands to her face. He tore them away, and slapped her again. "Bitch! Bitch! he cried through clenched teeth, his face twisted with pain. He tore the robe away from her. Now she was naked before him. He was insane with fury. "I'll fix your wagon!" He slapped her hard across the breasts. A shock of pain ran through her. She gasped and threw her arms around her breasts, to protect herself. He pummeled her arms with his fists. She jerked her body, throwing him off balance and kicked at his frenzied face. He tumbled over backwards. Norma lurched to her feet. Her screams rent the night. She ran. Barnes sprang up like a tiger and came after her. He tackled her, bringing her down again. Quickly he was over her, clawing and pounding, forcing her back against the grass.

"Now I'll have you, you little bitch!" he grunted. He held her by the throat, his thumbs pressing down until her chest swelled with pain and she gagged. One of his knees was jammed between her locked thighs. He took one hand away, easing the pressure off her throat, and he yanked at the zipper on his trousers.

"Norma! Norma! Where are you?"

She heard the deep-throated voice shout her name and a wave of hope spread over her. She whipped her head from his grasp. "Here!" she shouted. "Help!"

"Norma! Norma!"

She struggled with renewed strength, scratching at his evil face, biting and kicking. Barnes was determined to complete what he had started. Her nails raking his face only heightened his lust. Norma felt his wild, eager hands tearing at her thighs. She shifted her hips, turning on her side to protect herself.

Closer and closer, the grass-muted thud of running feet. "Norma! Where are you?" a voice called.

"Here! Here!" she screamed. "Here!" She was tiring. The rapist had turned her over. She could feel him against her. Never, never, she cried to herself. She would never yield. She strained her pelvic muscles, and smashed her fists into his face. A drivel of his spit ran from his mouth to her neck.

Then a dark figure towered over her. Barnes was suddenly lifted from her, cursing and struggling, but the tall figure held him away.

"You bastard!" It was Speed's angry voice.

Norma drew her naked body into a ball, clutching her legs. She began to sob brokenly. Her whole body was shaking.

She heard the sound of a fist slamming against bone and a startled cry of pain. "I'll kill you, you louse!" Another fist striking, the sound of the man scrabbling in the grass.

"She asked me to!" Barnes wailed. "She told me to meet her!" The hard toe of a boot thudding against ribs. "Stop it! She made me, I tell ya!" Sam squealed, his words spilling out with his gasping breath. "You don't know! She's screwing everybody in the damn show!"

"Get up!" Speed leaned over and dragged Barnes to his feet. He drove his fist into his face, holding him, cutting off his words. He hit him again and then released him. Barnes fell sprawling. Then he scrambled away and ran wildly without looking back.

"Speed," Norma whimpered. "Speed."

Kneeling next to her, Speed lifted her shoulders. He brushed the hair from her bruised face. She cried softly, her shoulders trembling. "Speed." She could think of nothing more to say and she repeated his name over and over, the relief flooding her, feeling safe in his embrace.

"You're okay," he said. "You're okay now."

"Speed, it's not true. What he said isn't true."

"I know that. He's dirt. Just try to forget it."

"It's so awful."

"It won't happen again. I'll take care of you."

"Oh, Speed." She twisted until she was on her knees. She buried her face against his chest, clinging to him. His arms encircled her, holding her firmly. She lifted her tear-stained face to him and he bent down and kissed her lightly.

They knelt face-to-face in the middle of the field, the soft moonlight cloaking them, the sweet scents of the summer-brown matted grass rising to envelop them. They were silent, unmoving; two people finding themselves in their loneliness and yearning; the mixture of relief and the will to belong to one another spreading between them until that realization that has driven man to woman for countless centuries seemed to inundate them, and their breath and pulse-beat flowed together, and it became difficult for either to breathe.

"Norma," he whispered. "I love you."

She did not answer. She took a deep breath and expired it shakily. She bowed her head and the tears rolled over her cheeks. It was too late. There was Lee. No matter what she felt now, she knew that nothing would matter the moment Lee touched her, because she was a slave to his sexual attraction. It was as though she were two people. The decent girl who found comfort and refuge in Speed's arms and knew that he was what she wanted, that she wanted to belong to him and be a part of his life; and the girl who was all physical and reacted to Lee's touch like a wanton harlot.

"Norma, I want you to …"

She pressed a finger to his lips, silencing him. She shook her head slowly, and agonized yearning was deep in her large, dark eyes.

"Please don't say it, Speed," she whispered, her voice choked.

"I can't help it," he said.

"Don't. Please."

"I love you. Doesn't that mean anything to you?"

She breathed deeply and bit down on her lip. It meant everything to her. But it was too late. She had to stop him from being hurt.

"No, it doesn't," she said softly, hating the words as they came off her lips, but knowing that it was the right thing to say. Speed was too good for her now. He was fine and clean, but she was soiled and dirty.

His breath came in sharply. Hurt showed on his face. His hands slid away from her and fell to his sides. He did not speak.

She fought back the impulse to retract the words. Maybe it wasn't too late. But it was. This she knew.

Rising slowly to her feet, she stood over him. The robe was open and her oiled body glistened in the moonlight, tawny and voluptuous.

She looked down at his bowed, kneeling figure with sadness, and she knew suddenly that she had reached maturity; that she was a woman, no longer a girl. She could never offer him a love that would be soiled.

"Speed," she said. He did not answer, made no movement. "Speed, look at me."

He lifted his head. The pain in his eyes wrenched at her heart. But she was determined that he should not love her.

"I can't love you," she said, fighting to keep her voice steady. She shrugged her shoulders and the white robe fell at her ankles. The moonlight shadowed the hollows of the flawless body, highlighted the high, jutting breasts that were melon-round and rigid. It shone on the flat plane of her stomach and the rich swell of her hips. It glistened on her long, smooth thighs. "But you can have me," she said, "If you want. Any time you want, Speed, any time!"

The line of his square jaw stiffened. He closed his eyes and his chin dropped to his chest. His fists clenched until the muscles of his forearms were knotted. He shook his head, "No, Norma! Not this way," he managed. "I'm not an animal."

"I'm sorry," she said in a voice that was barely audible. She walked away from the robe, leaving it in a crumpled heap before him. She crossed the field, her shoulders slumped, the warm night her shroud, the moonlight glittering on her naked body, not caring who saw her, the ache gnawing at her. All she knew was that she was walking away from him, the man she loved, because there was another man for whom she lusted. "Oh God," she prayed silently. "Kill me."

CHAPTER ELEVEN

The carney rolled. Headlights slanting across the dull black macadam. Road dust boiling from under the heavy double wheels, whipping the refuse and sailing it with the gravel, high and wide into the scrabble-grass dark, to settle and be still. Single-file, the tail-lights like the red eyes of ungainly sputtering beasts racing through the night.

Tired bodies swaying and jouncing on hard-spring seats, blood-shot eyes fixed to the white line, callous-hard hands grippng and twisting the black wheels. Sleeping with heads swaying and banging against the windows and awakening with the rude jolt of mid-west railroad tracks.

Kankakee. Morning mist. The disheveled, trampled plot of dust and crab-grass; the cans and debris of the last show. The stake man and his crew waiting in the half-light, tired and bearded. "She's all staked out. You can start shaking canvas right away."

"Okay, okay, Harry swing those trucks around on the right. Let's get it rolling."

No sleep. The ring of mallets on iron spikes. The groan of ropes on the block and tackle, grunting men, the dull rustle of spreading canvas, the whine and sputter of the gasoline generator. The sun slides over the flat east, eery and warming. The cock crow, the quickening traffic on the nearby road, necks craning from the passing cars. The tops are spread, the poles like spindly legs, then clothed with the side canvas. The carney all in place. The people sleeping through the sun-hot day, roasting under canvas, in metal trailers, in the backs of trucks. Then night.

"Hurry, hurry, hurry! Step right up and see the sights that your eyes have never before beheld. Hyah! Hyah! See the seven wonders of the world! See it! See it! See it!"

Running west, the carney rolled. Taylorville, Morrisburg, Cluney Falls, Bethany, Chillicothe, Kearnyville. One-night, two-night, three-night stands. Tear down and roll through the night, canvas spreading under the still dawn.

Kirkland's World of Wonder. Auspices Tall Cedars of Lebanon, Pioneer Sons of Haber County, Loyal Order of the Moose, Hokesville Volunteer Fire Company.

Hawking, grinding, sweating, swearing. Throat-rasping dust of the red Missouri clay when the sun beat down baking the midway. Mud that seeped and clogged and clung, when the skies opened up the rains, poured down. Cursing, bellowing, scheming, praying, the carney rolled. It blared into the stolid show-me towns like a honky-tonk messiah, bringing relief from the TV and the corner movie, lights and rowdy noise and when-I-was-a-kid memories, the chance to win the cupie doll, to ride the ferris wheel and the whirl-o-plane, to see the woman who fondles those reptiles the way a mother would fondle her baby, it came in the night—Coney Island on Wheels. Then it slipped away in the night, rumbling south, the red and gold trucks streaked with dust; leaving the footworn field of pop-corn boxes and plastic ice cream spoons to show where it had been.

Norma danced. She had forgotten how many times she had mounted the steps from the dressing tent and come down the ramp to whirl around the brazier of fire. The dance had been per-fected to the point where she was no longer emotionally affected by the primitive beat or the sensuous gyrations. But she had changed. Now she made the dance a sexual experience through careful planning of every step and motion of her hands and body. It was calculated to stimulate the male audience. This in itself created a cold veneer about her, and a growing loathing for the audience. She had fast become disenchanted with the glitter of the carney.

Since the closing night at Bloomington, Speed had kept his distance. She saw him, of course, because they were thrown together by the close proximity of the carney life, but he maintained a reserve that was at first heart-rending to her, but something she accepted as natural as the weeks passed. He was noticeably withdrawn and somber, and she could tell that his feeling for her had changed but little, but she maintained her aloofness.

Della was friendly, but Norma sensed a resentment in her that was confusing. Time refused to wear the edge off Della's pointed remarks concerning Lee Harker.

And Lee. Norma had relinquished any thoughts of combating his obvious domination over her. Although she knew that she could continue to dance without him, she still realized that she was his creation. There was a wide gulf between the girl who had run away from her home and the girl who now danced under the name of Tamara—and Lee filled the gulf. The affair was still a furtive-nocturnal thing, with Lee coming to her in the trailer while Darla was absent. The rest of the time he treated her the same as anyone else. At first this had bothered her, but this too she accepted. She felt that in his own strange way Lee was in love with her and that there was no one else for him. There was nothing she could do to make herself repel him, so she simply took things the way they were.

The dance of the flames had become the feature of the show, and in the six weeks since she first danced, Ed Kirkland had tripled her salary. While she steadily became bored with the carny and weary under the hardships of the exhausting schedule, she also realized that there was no other way that she could make as much money.

Rolling in from the north, the carny set up for a week at the Washaw County Fair. Shade trees dotted the parking area for the trailers, and there were terminals for electricity, running water, and permanent laundry sheds. The grass was green and well-tended. The weary carney settled down as though they had found the promised land.

When Norma returned to the dressing tent after her first show of the evening, a boy brought her a folded note. He stood, with wide-eyes taking in the half-naked girls, waiting for his answer. Norma unfolded the note. *I would like to see you on a business matter. Where and when would it be convenient? Frank Marco.*

Norma furrowed her brow thoughtfully. She tapped her fingers with the paper.

"Who gave you this?" she asked the boy.

"Man out there. Said to bring an answer."

"Tell him I'll see him here."

"Okay."

The boy slipped through the canvas and Norma dropped the note on the dressing table. She stared into the mirror and ran a finger lightly under her eyes. Her growing fatigue was beginning to show in slight shadows. She went to a folding chair and settled into it, crossing her legs.

"Smoke?" Darla asked, holding out a package of cigarettes. Norma took one and caught the book of matches which Darla tossed into the air. "Thanks," Norma said.

She lit the cigarette and leaned her head back, expelling the smoke towards the peaked top of the tent.

"If it gets any hotter in these damn towns I'm gonna melt," Lolly Lane complained.

"Like the proverbial witches tit," Darla said.

"Did you see that big stud up close to the platform?" Lolly said.

"Did I!" Darla exclaimed. "He must be hung like a stallion."

"Well, he's mine," Lolly said.

"You can have him," Darla said. "I like 'em smaller and better dressed. They got more dough and the plumbing stays in better order."

"Gawd!" Peggy said, tossing her fur neckpiece. "The way you talk. That must be a damned cash register you got in your belly."

"If ya got the cash you ring the bell."

The girls laughed. Norma only half-listened to the talk. It was usually the same, and she found it boring. They talked about men and sex and money. The tenor of the talk was generally irreverent and ribald. This, she now realized, was a natural effect of being a stripper with the carny. On the platform they showed their bodies to men who paid to see it. The dances were imitations of the sex act. The men they saw after the show were only interested in their bodies and the gratification of their sexual desires. Most of the men with the carny—excepting the roughnecks—were married. There was no chance for the girls to meet any other type of male except those who came for the obvious reasons. It warped their thinking until they had no idea that there was anything else.

I'm not a damn bit better than they are, Norma thought, drawing on the cigarette. The difference was that she wanted something better. The carny had been a refuge to her and she had found friends in Gus and Ed Kirkland, but she knew that she wanted more. There was a life that was beyond the canvas boundaries and she wanted to taste it. There were times when she thought of California and all that it had once meant to her. She recalled the photos of the small modern houses nestled in the foothills—houses that were homes and where families lived and grew and sank roots. Families. She had never really been part of a family, not the kind of family you might want to be a part of. This was a void in her life and it was gradually becoming a hunger. She realized that she could never imagine herself and Lee being a family. Speed, yes, but that was a forgotten thought.

A handsome, well-groomed head appeared in the canvas opening. "Sorry," he said, "There was no place to knock." His smile showed a row of even white teeth. "My name is Frank Marco."

The girls turned their attentions to him and Darla whistled softly.

"Come in," Norma said, rising to her feet. "I'm Norma Chiari."

His smile broadened and he entered the tent. "Ah, an Italiano."

"More or less," Norma said. He glanced at the girls and Norma said, "Darla, Lolly, Peggy and Bertha."

"My pleasure." He turned back to Norma. "I am sorry to be so secretive with my note, but I am on an errand of piracy, and Ed Kirkland would scalp me if he knew I was here."

"Oh?"

He sat on the edge of a theatrical trunk. The girls regarded him with curiosity, but he kept his frankly admiring gaze on Norma. He made a gesture towards her chair and Norma sat down. "I just caught your act," he said. "You're terrific."

"Thank you."

"I came some distance to see you. Some friends of mine saw you dance and told me about you. Everything they said was true."

Norma arched her brow quizzically. Plenty of the patrons of the show had tried to date her before, but none of them had started quite like this.

"Now I'll get to the point," Marco said. "I own a club called The Paradise. It's a pretty swank joint just south of St. Louis. I want you to work for me. I'll pay you three-fifty a week."

Norma blinked. His offer registered slowly. "Are you kidding?" she asked.

"I didn't come all the way from St. Louis to make jokes. I'm serious. I brought a contract with me."

Stunned, Norma turned and looked at the other girls. They were open-mouthed with surprise.

"What do you say?" Marco asked.

"I don't know," Norma said. "I'll have to think about it."

"I'm driving back in the morning," Marco said. "Remember, the carny season only lasts another month. This is a regular spot."

"I'll have to talk with Ed Kirkland," Norma said.

Marco laughed. "He'd be crazy to let you go." He pulled a white card from his pocket. "Tell you what," he said. "Here's my card. I'll be at the Plaza Hotel in town here until morning. You think it over and call me. If you want to finish out the season with Kirkland, okay. You can open at my place when you're done, or next week which I'd like better. Either way you got a solid offer." He got to his feet, smoothing out the suit of pale Hongkong silk that draped perfectly on his short, stocky body. Everything about him was expensive and carefully tailored. He was black-haired and swarthily handsome and he carried himself confidently, straight as a rod. "That's more than we ever paid a dancer at my place," he said. "And if you're a smart girl you can make a lot more than that."

"I'll call you," Norma said.

He reached out and shook her hand. "I hope you decide to drive back with me," he said. He smiled around the tent and left.

Norma stared down at his card and there was a long moment of silence.

"Wow!" Darla said. "Why don't I ever find somebody like that?"

"Whatta ya gonna do, kid?" Darla asked, excited.

"Talk to Ed Kirkland," Norma said.

"You don't expect Kirkland to tell you to leave, do you? Holy cow, he's making a bundle outta you right now. He'll bust a gut if you leave."

"Screw him," Peggy said. "Think of the three and a half bills a week, and no traveling. Two or three shows a night. No dust and no mud, and air conditioning." She gave a deep sigh. "Hey, maybe you'll need a maid. Keep me in mind."

Norma was determined to speak with Kirkland. The offer had come as a complete surprise and it was still too new to her to really know what to think of it. She owed a great deal to Kirkland. Even if she accepted the offer, he would have to know about it in advance. But more important was Lee. Frank Marco had seemed so eager to hire her that he would surely include Lee and the combo in the deal if she insisted. Would he be glad? She felt certain that he would. He never had a good thing to say for the carny. This could be the thing that might bring them closer together. She wanted more than a sexual relationship, and this might be the opportunity for them. She wanted to run out and speak with him at once, but she heard Wendall begin the grind for the next show.

When the show ended Norma waited until the patrons had filed from the tent, then she slipped through the opening to speak with Lee. He was getting up from his drums and turning towards the entrance when she came onto the platform.

"Lee."

"Huh? Oh, it's you."

"Lee, I want to talk to you a minute."

"Later, huh?" He waved a hand and walked away.

"Lee," she said to his back. "This is important."

"It'll keep. I wanna catch a beer," he said without looking back.

Watching him go, her face reddened with sudden shame and anger. What made him act like that? She whirled and stalked up the ramp, but by the time she had reached the dressing tent she had rationalized his actions, feeling that something was bothering him, and that he would react favorably to the news after the final show when they could be alone.

The night pressed long and the completion of each show was a relief. She thought hard about Frank Marco's offer. It was strange to her now that she had never before thought of what she was going to do when the show ended for the season. The opportunity to dance in a night club and at a good salary worked a change in her thinking. In the past the future had always been something to dream about, but there was never anything real about the dreams. Now there was a future in front of her and the decision to reach out for it was both frightening and overpowering. Now she wondered if the carny had really toughened her as much as she had thought. She had to take stock of her position and her feelings. The show had been boring her, but now that she was faced with the possibility of leaving it, the carny seemed like more of a home than ever.

She came off the ramp for the last time that night with a deep sigh of relief. Only Lolly was left in, the dressing tent, and she was bent close to the mirror taking special care with her make-up. Norma was in a hurry to change, but she could not help but pause and glance at Lolly. The girl's dress was more elaborate than usual. Her hair was swept up on the back of her head, and she wore a white linen dress that clung to her body like an extra layer of skin. The top of the dress was low and the tight bodice pressed upwards to make hillocks of her breasts. White heels gave her a long-limbed grace. Norma never before had noticed how pretty the girl was, and it surprised her.

"Must be a big date tonight," Norma said.

"Special special," Lolly said, holding up crossed fingers.

"Well, good luck," Norma said.

"Thanks." She worked her lips together to spread the lipstick evenly. She gathered up her purse. "I'm all butterflies," she said. "This was the last thing in the world I expected and now I'm scared to death I'll say all the wrong things." She shook her head and dashed out of the tent.

Norma swung her arms out of the blue silk robe which covered her and hung it on a pole. She unhooked the grass skirt, folded it carefully and put it in a trunk. With a heavy towel, she rubbed the oil off her body, working quickly; impatient to see Lee and tell him the news. Usually, she removed most of the make-up from her face, but this time she merely tied her hair back with a ribbon and began to dress; pulling the slacks over her legs, working her feet into the loafers. She tugged her bra into place, cinched it at the back, then slipped into a white shirt that she buttoned quickly and tied the tails at her waist.

Hurrying up the steps, she slipped through the canvas to the main tent. It was already darkened.

She went down the ramp to the platform and jumped to the ground. She went to the entrance and Wendall was sweating over the final count of the tickets.

"You see Lee?"

"Uh?" Wendall looked up, breathing with his usual labored wheeze. "Oh." He glanced around. "He was here a minute ago. Oh, yeah, he went off towards the end of the midway."

"Thanks."

She walked the length of the glittering horse shoe. The ferris wheel was motionless, but still lighted, and the operator was tinkering with the engine.

"Hey, Benny."

"What?" The small, balding man looked up from his work. "Oh, hi, Norma."

"Seen Lee?"

"Yeah. A few minutes ago. He walked over that way." He pointed off into the dark where a dense stand of trees was outlined against the sky. Norma had been there earlier in the day. There was a small stream that tumbled off a hill, rushing over stones and rocks, and through the group of trees. She rejoiced. It was a beautiful spot and Lee had probably gone there to relax. She could not have imagined a better place to talk to him.

Ducking under a rope, she squeezed between two trucks and walked quickly. She found the path that ran to the place and she followed it. Away from the lights she had to slow down to stay on the path. She walked two hundred yards until she reached the first trees and she stopped.

There was the sound of voices ahead. Muted, but unmistakably the voices of two people. Norma tensed. Her breath came more quickly and her own heart beat was loud to her ears. She took a step forward, afraid of what she might find, but drawn forward by a gnawing curiosity. When she recognized the voices she stopped. Della and Lee. What were they doing together, these two, who hated each other so deeply. She moved cautiously a step at a time. Her eyes were accustomed to the dark. She stepped off the path, and mounted a small rise so that she stood between two thick trees and looked down into the small, grassy clearing at the edge of the stream, where she had sat in the afternoon.

Moonlight filtering through the trees cast a pale light on the clearing. Della was lying on her back, her hair spread around her head, her arms spread. One leg was straight out and the other was bent at the knee, throwing her full skirt high on her thighs. Lee sat next to her with his back to the trees where Norma leaned heavily and watched, transfixed.

"We never get together enough," Della said.

"It ain't easy," Lee said.

"You'd have more time if you wasn't always after that kid."

"Let's not talk about her," Lee said.

"It burns me," Della said. She twisted and her hand moved out over his legs. "I'm greedy. I want this all for me."

"How about Gus?"

She dropped back and flung her arm out. "Hell, if Gus gets it up once a month he's lucky."

They both laughed. Lee reached out and ran his hand over the twin peaks of Della's big breasts.

"Goodie," Della said huskily. "I like this when I start to go crazy inside, and I don't do anything about it." Lee closed his hand tightly and her breath came in sharply. Norma knew how it felt, because he often did it to her.

Lee unbuttoned Della's blouse. Norma felt a compulsive urge to watch the careful procedure she knew so well.

"Slowly," Della whispered in a great gust of passion. "I like it slow." The blouse parted. Norma saw the other woman's breasts rise sharply. The dark-tinted nipples were as big as quarters. Lee pulled up the skirt, exposing the big white thighs.

"Don't you ever wear anything underneath?" he asked.

"Not when I'm gonna meet you. I know you're always in a hurry, Lee."

Della shrugged the blouse from her shoulders. She reached down to unfasten the skirt and kicked it off. She leaned back. Cupping a breast with one hand, she reached up and pulled his head down. Her hand slid over him and under the waistband of his trousers. "Come on baby," she crooned, "Mama's got it for you!"

Pushing against him, Della pressed him down. He lifted his head like a child suckling, and her fingers went over the buttons of the shirt. She squirmed, laughing lightly, pulling his shirt away. She loosened his belt. Lee did not move, letting her tug the trousers away from his hips.

Della pulled off Lee's shoes and they were both naked, their bodies white and macabre as they clung together on the grass.

Norma turned and ran, plunging into the dark, the lights of the midway before her. The tears streamed over her face.

She noticed Wendall at the counter of the lunch concession and she ran there.

"Wendall," she said through labored breathing. "Where's Speed?"

He stared at her with surprise. "He went into town with Lolly," he said.

Norma's face went white. Too late, too late! She seemed to die inside and her shoulders slumped. Without speaking she turned and walked away. She moved with shuffling steps, her senses numbed.

CHAPTER TWELVE

Norma glanced around the empty lobby of the hotel while the desk clerk consulted his register. She was annoyed by the prissy man's suspicious air, but she knew it was the heavy make-up on her face that made him that way.

"Five-o-seven," the clerk said. "Use the house phone over there."

"Come in, come in. What a pleasant surprise." Frank Marco was wearing a silk brocade robe with a white silk scarf at his neck. His hair was wet from a recent combing.

It was the usual impersonal hotel room with the blonde fur-niture, the writing desk with green blotter, the large mirror over the dresser, the two straight-backed chairs, the one easy chair with the cigarette burns, the small tray and whiskey bottle, the two glasses, the ice.

Going straight to the easy chair, Norma sat down. She had changed into a clinging white dress, and when she sat, it whis-pered on the nylon stockings and stretched taut about her thighs. She crossed her legs and leaned back. Frank Marco still stood by the closed door.

"I have decided to accept your offer, Mr. Marco," she said. "I'll drive back with you, if it's okay."

He cocked an eyebrow slightly, surprised at the sudden change in her, noticing that she was suddenly bitter. She was obvi-ously disturbed about something. "I'll get the contract," he said.

"Can you get me a room here for tonight? I already left the show. I can pick up my bag there in the morning."

"Sure thing," he said. "I'll call the desk." He brought the folded paper from his closet and spread it on the desk. "You can look this over and sign at the bottom."

Norma heaved out of the chair and leaned over the desk. She knew that Marco was looking at her closely and that his eyes were traveling over her body. She didn't care. She read the part that mentioned the salary and where it said that she would do only two shows a night. She took the pen up and signed her name. Marco reached down to pick up the contract. His arm brushed against her breast and she knew that it was intentional.

"Now let's have a drink," he said jovially.

"Thank's, I'd love one" Norma said. She had never graduated from the beer at Darla's, but now she wanted a drink. She went back to the chair and sat down, crossing her legs again.

"You take water?"

Yes," she said, because she had heard other people say they wanted water and she didn't want Marco to know that she had never had a drink of whiskey.

Marco went into the bathroom with the two glasses and she heard the tap run. He came back into the room, crossed over and handed her a glass. He held out his glass and she mimicked his gesture. He clinked the glasses.

"To the new Tamara!" he said.

"And the new Norma," she muttered. She looked at Frank Marco and she smiled for no reason. It made her feel good and she laughed.

"What's so funny he inquired?"

"I feel good," Norma said, giggling. The warmth had spread over her completely. She lifted the glass and drained it again, then reached and poured more whiskey from the bottle. She settled back and kicked off her shoes. She tried to think about Della and Lee, but now the whole thing was funny to her. She laughed. "Awful!" she said.

"What's awful?" Frank Marco asked. His voice was composed and he watched her carefully.

"Them two," Norma said, waving the glass. "On the grass. Like dogs. And Gus don't even know." She laughed again and brought the glass up, spilling some of the liquor as she drank.

Lowering the glass, the humor suddenly left everything. She took a deep breath and sighed. The fingers relaxed on the glass and it fell to the carpet. The room began to tilt. She gritted her teeth. Something was wrong, "Ohhh," she groaned. Her hands held tightly to the arms of the chair. She stared at Marco and saw him in duplicate. She felt strange.

It had been only a half hour since her first drink, but the combination of exhaustion and an empty stomach and the emotional instability was too much.

The room reeled. Her eyes were wide and she stared at the bathroom door. It seemed to be a mile away. A wave of nausea roiled through her. The ceiling and walls spun and the door seemed out of reach. She lurched to her feet. She staggered, hitting the bed, then the desk. She leaned forward, hoping that the momentum would carry her. She could not feel her legs, but she was moving. The bathroom door at last. She slammed through. She dropped to her knees over the commode, gripping the porcelain edges. She heaved painfully. When the contracting spasms were over, she laid her cheek against the cool porcelain and sighed. She did not want to move. It was so cool, and she was too warm. She forced herself to her feet and ran water from the tap. She washed her face. When she looked up into the mirror she groaned. The heavy makeup was smeared and streaked and she was a grotesque mask. She took the small bar of soap and the wash cloth and washed the make-up away. She dried her face with a towel, leaving the traces of make-up on the towel. She glanced into the mirror, then closed her eyes.

Drunk, she muttered. I'm drunk. She shook her head. She was so warm, too warm. She opened her eyes and turned her head. There was the shower. She sighed. The shower. That would be cool. Her hands went to the zipper of the tight dress.

She removed her clothes, letting each article drop as it came off. She was cooler and the tile felt good against her bare feet. She stumbled to the stall shower, leaned against the wall and turned on the water. It streamed out with a rush and she put her hand under it. Cold! She turned the other handle until the shock was taken off the water. She stepped into the stall and gasped as the water struck her. She leaned back against the tile wall and the jets peppered her breasts, the water streaming down over her loins. It felt so good.

"That feel better?"

She turned her head and Frank Marco stood beyond the shower entrance. She stretched her arms languidly. "Wonderful," she said. The world seemed cool and rosy. She would stay under the water the rest of the night. Everything was wonderful. She closed her eyes. The jets of water stung her breasts, but the sensation was not unpleasant. She sensed movement and she opened her eyes. Frank Marco was coming into the stall with her. She giggled. He was close to her and the water sprayed off his shoulders. She noticed the dark matting of hair on his body.

Why was Frank Marco in the shower with her? He must be warm and wanted to cool off. But he was shutting the water away from her. She reached out and turned him away. The jets hammered at her breasts again. Felt so good. She closed her eyes and sighed. Her eyes blinked open when Marco touched her. She began to lift her hands defensively, but she saw that he had the soap in his hand and he was only helping her. His body shielded her from the stream of water again, but he was soaping her and it didn't matter. She watched the suds growing on her breasts, and the soap slid over her, over and under and between the breasts. She sighed heavily. He was so nice to her, so helpful. A feeling of well-being enveloped her. The soap slid over her belly in circular motions, over her hips and thighs. She leaned her head back against the tile and enjoyed the gently massaging fingers.

She opened her eyes suddenly. He had her wedged in the corner, and the wet mat of hair on his chest was rubbing against her breasts.

"Oh No!" She began to struggle instinctively. Her body was slippery with soap and he had difficulty holding her. She gripped his hips to keep him away. They slammed against the walls of the small enclosure. The water roared down on them. Frank Marco was grunting and pushing, his hands and body holding her back. She had to keep her feet spread to maintain her balance.

She was facing the stall opening. Heaving away from the wall, she threw herself forward. In his mounting passion, he was unconscious of balance. He went over backwards. Still joined, they fell through the opening. Marco's shoulders slammed against the tile floor. Norma felt a blinding stab of pain as she wrenched free of him, carried forward by the momentum of the fall. Her hands went out to break her fall and she sprawled, sliding over him, and rolled against the wall.

Marco cursed, his voice a tight snarl. She gained her feet and ran, her wet feet slipping. His hand flashed out and hit her ankle. She stumbled, still running and fell through the doorway onto the carpet of the room. She regained her feet.

He came after her like a madman, snarling, running crouched, his eyes wild, his body dripping, the black hair plastered over his forehead. He slammed into her, carried her back and flung her down on to the bed, throwing himself over her. His precise manner, his sauvity, were gone. Gasping for breath, dripping wet, he was all lust.

Norma kicked and struggled, inching back along the bed, but he was strong and he held her down. Her head touched the headboard. She was losing her strength. One of her flaying hands touched an ash tray on the night table. Her fingers closed over the thick edges. She lifted it. It was heavy glass.

She looked down. His face was buried between her breasts. The black hair glistened under the glare of the ceiling light. Her arm rose — the light danced on the prisms of the glass for the fraction of a second — and fell, driving the dull point of the receptable into the base of the skull.

His breath whistled out like a balloon deflated — a whoosh! His back arched and trembled. Her hand rose and fell. The sound was a dull thud as bone gave way. His fingers tightened, digging into the flesh of her shoulders.

Lifting her hand, she stared at the ash tray. It glistened with red and bristled with hair. She shook it loose from her stiff fingers and it fell to the bed, blotting the white coverlet with red. Her breathing was slow and tight. She touched her fingers to his shoulders as though she might be expecting an electric shock. She pushed slowly, sliding her body away.

The thing rolled and left her and sprawled across the bed. The arms were outflung. The head dropped over the edge of the bed. Blood ran from the lower corner of the open mouth and the startled eyes stared at the ceiling. The legs were akimbo.

The nausea left her and the shock began to subside. He was dead. She had killed him! It was like an echo in her brain. Killed him! Killed! Killed!

She looked down at the blood that covered her and she shrank back as though she might get away from it. She was sticky with blood and hair and the soap.

Killed him! Killed him! What would they do to her? Her heartbeat increased and fear assailed her. Murder!

Terrified, she lurched from the bed and ran to the bathroom to get her clothes. The tile was cool to her feet and she shuddered with remembrance. When she dipped her hand down to lift her bra she saw the hand covered with blood. She had to wash. She looked up. The shower was still running. She straightened and walked to the stall entrance with reluctance. She stopped before the opening. There is a man dead in the other room, her mind said. You cannot calmly wash the blood from you in this shower where it all began. There was nothing else to do. The urge for self-preservation overwhelmed the moral objections. She stepped into the water.

Get a hold on yourself. It wasn't your fault. You fought back, that's all. But I killed him! I killed him!

She forced herself into the room. The body was there as she knew it would be, naked and grotesque; the white coverlet sodden with the blood. She skirted the bed, keeping against the wall, never once taking her eyes from the body. Her foot touched a shoe. She looked down and then picked up the shoes one at a time and put them on her feet. She lifted her purse from the desk. The contract! It had her name on it and she had almost forgotten it! What had he done with it? Her eyes flew around the room wildly. She saw it folded on the top of the dresser. She crossed over and snatched it up, opening her purse she jammed it inside. She went around the bed again. She had to pass the face to reach the door. The eyes were wide and staring and they seemed to be accusing. Her back rubbed against the wall as she edged past. Her hand touched the doorknob and she turned it slowly, pulling the door open.

A round red light at the end of the hall said: EXIT. She walked quickly towards it. Pushing through the metal door, she found herself in a fire tower. The stairs were concrete and steel. Without a pause, she started down, the clack of her heels echoing up through the dimly-lighted gray cavern of steps. The sound was maddening. She stopped and removed her shoes. She ran down the steps counting off the floors. Four, three, two, one. She was breathing heavily. She put the shoes back on and went to the doorway. The knob did not turn. She pushed against it. She rattled the knob. It was locked.

Tears welled in her eyes. A feeling of hopelessness surged over her. She went to the door that opened on to the lobby. There was a small glass pane and she peered through it. The lobby was half-lighted and silent. There was the only the steady clatter of an adding machine. The clerk was working on the daily receipts. She eased the swinging door open, praying that the hinges were oiled. She slipped through and pressed against the wall.

Still holding her shoes, she edged across the carpet, her eyes on the lighted desk. She could make out the top of the clerk's head. He was seated, his back to her. The machine clattered. She thought that he would surely hear her breathing. She was in the middle of the lobby.

The elevator whirred, coming down. Her heart leaped. She looked up at the floor gauge. The metal needle turned slowly, but steadily. The adding machine clattered. The clerk yawned aloud and stretched his arms. He was going to stand!

She walked, slowly, then faster. She knew that she should look straight ahead and just keep going, but she could not tear her eyes from the clerk's back. He settled in the chair and rubbed his eyes. The front door was standing open. For the first time she was thankful of the heat. The elevator clanged. But the sound was behind her and she was on the sidewalk and hurrying away.

Once past the hotel, she stopped and put the shoes on. She took a deep breath and hurried, her stride as long as the spike heels would permit.

There were two cabs parked before an all-night restaurant, the drivers sitting on the fenders talking.

"I'd like a cab," she said. The moment the words left her lips she knew that it was the wrong thing. The drivers would certainly remember her. But it was too late now.

"Take your pick," one of the drivers said.

She opened the rear door of the nearest cab and slidslid inside. The driver came around and got in behind the wheel.

"The station," she said quickly.

"Right."

The cab eased away from the curb and rolled along the silent street.

"Would you know if there is a train for St. Louis?" she asked.

"Not at this hour," the driver said over his shoulder. "The first one out of here is at seven."

"What time is it?" she asked.

The man checked his watch. "Three-thirty," he said.

"I have to get to St. Louis," she said. "Is there a bus running?"

"Greyhound runs all night," he said.

"Take me there," she said.

"Okay." The cab slowed and the driver made a U-turn. He went a block and made a left turn.

A blue and white sign blinked GREYHOUND and the legs of the white dog flickered back and fourth. The cab slid up to the curb and the driver reached out and stopped the meter. Norma glanced at the fare. She reached into her purse and gave the driver a five dollar bill. Opening the door, she said, "Thanks," and leaped out.

"Thank *you!*" the driver said, staring at the bill.

Norma crossed the walk and pushed through the glass door. There were half-a-dozen people in the waiting room. A pinball machine rang out. From the lunch counter behind the glass wall to the left, the juke box was groaning with a simpering male voice. The eyes of the sitting people followed her across the tile floor. She stopped at the ticket counter. The clerk looked up from his desk. He came to his feet and walked to the counter.

"Yes," he said, his eyes lowered to the deep-valleyed expanse of breast that showed above the top of the white dress.

"I want a one-way to St. Louis," she said.

She paid, took her change and the ticket. "When does the next bus leave?

He glanced up at the clock on the wall. "It's due in here in fifteen minutes. There's a ten-minute stop."

The desk clerk would remember her, the tight white dress and the full-curved body, the black hair. The cab driver would remember the large tip and that she was in a hurry to get to St. Louis. The ticket clerk would remember what he had seen. So far, her trail would end at the bus station. A sexy-looking girl in a white dress in a hurry to get to St. Louis.

CHAPTER THIRTEEN

The moon seemed to lose its intensity as the sky began to pale. When she saw the buildings of the fair grounds, Norma stepped off the highway and started on an angle across the fields. Stooping through a barbed-wire fence, she snagged her dress. It tore as she pulled away, but she didn't care. She had begun to hate the dress. It was designed to attract attention and it had already forced her into alleys, behind bushes and into ditches, to avoid the lights of approaching automobiles.

She reached the trailer where she knew Della would be sleeping. She gritted her teeth and moved past. She circled the trailers, avoiding the trucks and the sleeping men. She came around until the circular motordrome was before her. Slipping under a wall of canvas, she went to the small trailer where Speed lived. She stopped and took a deep breath. Would Lolly be in Speed's bed? Her fingers tensed, squeezing the leather of her shoes. Sex, sex, sex. God, did the whole world revolve on sex? Was there anything else? She reached out, her hand touching the side of the trailer and she closed her eyes. She saw a vivid scene, a dark hole that gradually lightened until she saw at the bottom a mass of twisting, writhing bodies, legs and arms entwined like undulating rope. Everyone she knew gasping and panting and groveling in a orgy of sex. Then the whole scene was suddenly blotted with blood, the thick red substance rising and bubbling up, topped with a ghastly froth; and one body rising out of the mass, standing waist-high in the flood, arms outstretched, large, high breasts dripping blood. It was herself.

She gasped, her eyes snapping open. She breathed quickly and unevenly. She threw herself against the trailer door and beat at it with the heel of her shoe.

"Speed!" she whispered hoarsely. "Speed! Speed!"

"Wha'?" The voice inside thick with sleep.

"Speed!" Her voice rose and died on a quick sob.

There was a scrambling sound and the thud of barefeet on the floor from within. The door clicked and pushed against her. Norma rolled away, leaning her shoulder against the trailer's side. The door swung open.

"Norma!" Speed wore the bottoms of pajamas. His chest was bare. His yellow hair was like a thatch on his head. His brow was deeply furrowed with concern.

She looked up at him with imploring, terror-stricken eyes. Speed jumped to the ground and gripped her elbows. "What's the matter?"

She shook her head, unable to speak. Her shoulders trembled under his grasp and tears streamed from her eyes and spilled over her cheeks. His eyes ran over her, taking in the torn dress, the hem fringed with mud. Her lips moved, but no sound came. He stooped and swung her up in his arms, grunting with the effort as he climbed through the small doorway into the trailer. He put her down on the bed that filled the one end. Then he closed the door. Coming back to her, he took one of her hands and held it tightly in both of his. "What happened?"

"I ... " Her eyes left him and she choked. She stared up at the ceiling and closed her eyes. "I killed a man." Her voice was rattled and quiet.

A stillness filled the small enclosure. Speed's grip tightened on her hand. She turned towards him and her eyes were wide. "Did you hear what I said?"

He nodded slowly, unable to believe. "I heard you," he whispered. His hard jaw jutted and his eyes were slits in his square face.

"I killed him." Her voice was slightly gagged, then it began to rise. "I killed him!" Her eyes suddenly flashed and the muscles of her throat tensed to scream. Speed clamped a hand over her mouth.

"Why did you decide so suddenly to take the job?" he asked.

She looked up at him and quickly lowered her eyes.

"Was it something to do with Lee?"

She nodded her head.

"What happened?"

"I ... I can't talk about that."

"You have to. I have to know everything if I'm going to be any help.

"I saw him with Della," she said. "They were ... I watched. I ... I stood there and watched them."

"And you decided to run away."

"I came to you," she said softly. "You weren't here. You were with ... with Lolly.

"I'm sorry. If I had known I would have been waiting."

"It's too late," she moaned. "It's always too late."

"It's not," he said. "We'll get out of this. Now let's see. There were enough people to identify you, but they wouldn't know who you were or where you came from. The business about St. Louis was quick thinking. This is just a jerkwater town and the cops won't be too sharp. They'll probably stop with the bus station and pass it on to the St. Louis cops."

"It will be in the papers," she said. "The other girls saw him in the tent."

"Yes," he mused. 'They might get it, but they're carny. They won't spill anything. It just isn't done in the carny. The cops would have to beat it out of them."

"I don't blame you, but you musn't show it." He gripped her shoulders. "The important thing is to act as though none of this has happened. You'll have to go through the day the way you would go through any other day. It's going to be rough at first, but this is one thing you'll have to do."

"I won't be able to dance."

"Yes you will. You'll have to dance."

"I'm afraid."

"Get some sleep. Poor kid, you must be dead."

She grabbed his hands. "Don't leave me. Speed, don't leave me alone. I can't stand to be alone. Please, Speed. I need you."

"I'll be right here." He took her hands away and placed them at her sides. He looked down at her and his expression was serious. "I love you, Norma."

Her breath caught and she bit her lip. She turned and buried her face in the tangle of bed covers. "And I had to bring you into this," she cried, the words muffled.

"I'm glad," he said.

"Oh, Speed, why did things have to be like this?"

"This can be just the beginning," he said.

CHAPTER FOURTEEN

The afternoon was fading and the sounds of the carny were blasting about her when she awoke. She came out of the deep sleep slowly, stretching with the somnolent motions of a cat. She lifted the long lashes of her eyes, still drugged. Then suddenly she remembered where she was and she snapped erect.

"Hi," Speed said. "Good sleep?"

She relaxed with a long, deep breath. He was standing over his small gas stove and the smell of hot coffee filled the trailer.

"I got you something to eat," he said. "How do you feel?"

"I feel better," she said.

"Good." He poured the coffee into a cup and brought it to her. She sat up on the bed, her legs curled under her. She took the coffee and sipped it.

"Sandwich," Speed said. "Ham."

"I'm starved."

Under the small talk her eyes were wandering. "It's over here," Speed said. He lifted the newspaper from the small table and snapped it open. He spread it before her. The headline was large and black.

"Frank Marco wasn't just anybody," Speed said. "It sounds as if you did the world a service."

She read the story hastily. A hotel maid had found the body. Marco was dead, his head beaten in. The night clerk and elevator operator told of a mysterious woman in white who went to the man's room at two-thirty a.m. There was a quote from the operator. "He knew the girl, because I saw her enter the room and he was awful glad to see her." There was a quote from the night clerk. "She wasn't anybody from town. The way she acted I would say she was a St. Louis prostitute." The rest of the story gave the impression that the killing was gangster vengeance, then it went on to tell about Frank Marco. Norma's eyes widened and she wondered what the job at The Paradise would have been like. Marco was a member of the national crime syndicate. He was alleged to be a mid-west fingerman for Murder Inc., was implicated in gambling, narcotics and wide-scale prostitution. It was rumored that the Kansas City mobsters were not on good terms with Marco. When she finished, Norma raised her eyes to Speed.

"If you're wondering why Marco came up here to see you himself," Speed said, "so am I."

"I don't understand."

"I can only figure this. He was a man who dealt in women. You're a pretty special female. I know that the syndicate supplies women to some bigwigs and they charge plenty for the right girl, and they keep it very quiet. If somebody big saw you and decided he wanted you, Marco might make the deal himself."

"It sounds unbelievable. But he wanted to hire me to dance."

"Would you have gone to his place for any other reason?"

"Certainly not."

"Then he had to offer you a job dancing. You might have danced, too, but for a mighty small audience. There wouldn't have been much you could do once you were settled in Marco's place. The mob has long tentacles and you wouldn't have left until they were ready for you to leave."

Norma shuddered. "I can hardly believe it," she said.

"Do you believe what happened last night? Two days ago you would have thought that pretty fantastic."

She looked down at the newspaper. "There's nothing about the cab driver or the bus station."

"They'll probably pick that up later. So far it sounds good. If they already think that it was someone from St. Louis or Kansas City, this will make it solid."

"But somebody must have known that he was coming here for me."

"On that we just cross our fingers and hope that it was somebody who would rather forget the whole thing."

Norma bit into the sandwich and chewed thoughtfully. They were silent and the carny sounds floated about them; the music of the merry-go-round, the shouts of the barkers, the squeals of women and children, the blare of the loudspeakers. The sun had gone down and the light was fading in the trailer.

"It still frightens me," she said.

"We just have to sweat it out. I have to go out and get the drome rolling. Kirkland is already wondering why I haven't been riding. You can stay here, but you better get out of that dress before you get ready to go on."

"I hate to have you away from me," she said.

"That I like to hear." He smiled. "But it will look better if we're both working."

"I know."

"There's more coffee there if you want it." He turned back when he touched the door handle. He looked up at her, saying nothing, then he opened the door and disappeared through it.

Norma finished the coffee, then she lifted the paper and read the story again. She threw the paper aside and leaned back in the bed. There was one thing she had not told Speed and remembering it sickened her. She could not rationalize in her mind what was going on in her body while she was killing Marco. She looked down along her body as though it did not belong to her, and her eyes narrowed with loathing. There had to be a reason that she was constructed in such a way that it brought out the lust in men. With smaller breasts, frailer hips and thinner legs, she might have been able to live a normal life without men crawling over her.

But there was Speed. He saw her body and he desired her. Norma had seen it plainly in his eyes. But he was different. When she looked at the body in that light—thinking of Speed—she was glad of the flawless perfection. But could she ever give herself to Speed? Would he want her if he knew how the body reacted to other men; that it was a wanton thing that could move separate from her mind; that even while she killed, the body sated itself on the nerve-torn corpse.

She twisted and muffled a sharp cry of despair. I am being punished! This is my purgatory! She lay, unmoving for a long time, then she arose and slipped her feet to the floor. She stood and looked down for her shoes. When she found them she put them on and left the trailer.

It was dark and she was in the shadows of the drome. The boards of the big barrel thundered and she heard the sharp stacatto of the exploding cylinders as the motorcycle roared around the inside of the drome. Looking up, she saw the backs of the people on the catwalk looking down. She slipped around the trailer and under the canvas barrier. She ran lightly across the grass, keeping into the shadows until she reached Darla's trailer. It was dark and she sighed with relief.

Inside the trailer she unzipped the dress and pulled it over her head. She rumpled it and stuffed it into the rear of a drawer. She put on a blouse and a full skirt and low-heeled shoes. She left the trailer and crossed the grass plot to the midway. She came under the canvas near the ferris wheel and she waved to Benny, the operator.

"Ed Kirkland's been looking for you," Benny called.

Norma's breath caught and her pulse quickened. What could he want? Had the police been there? She hurried toward the dressing tent. A hand caught her arm and a stifled cry left her throat. She whirled, her first thoughts to pull away and run. Gus was grinning at her, his homely, freckled face amused.

"You sure are goosey," Gus said.

Her breath came out with exaggerated gasps and she laughed. "You frightened me," she said.

"I didn't see you around today. I missed our talk."

"I'll make up for it tomorrow," she said. For weeks she had formed a habit of sitting around and talking to Gus. Actually, it was listening, but she enjoyed his stories and his warm, light humor. It made her slightly sad to think of Della and Lee, and what Gus might think. It made her dislike Della.

"Ed Kirkland's been looking for you," Gus said. "You better run over and see him before you go on."

The office wagon was directly across from where they were standing and it would be impossible to avoid seeing Kirkland without making an excuse.

"I'll see him," she said. She turned and crossed the midway, picking her way through the crowd. She mounted the side steps of the office wagon and knocked on the door.

"Come in!"

She opened the door and stepped inside. It was exactly the same as the first time she had entered here. Pearl at the counter with the wads of money, Kirkland behind his desk.

"You want to see me?" she asked.

"Oh, it's you. I was worried about you."

"Worried? Worried about what?"

Kirkland seemed flustered. He leaned back in his chair and made a waving gesture with his hands. "Just worried. You weren't around today, that's all."

"I'm okay," Norma said, trying to control her nervousness and making it more obvious.

Kirkland cocked his head and squinted. "You sure everything is okay, kid? If anything's bothering you, you can spill it to me, y'know."

"No, everything's fine." She knotted her hands together.

"If you say so, okay. I ain't trying to be nosey. I just ... well, I wanta be sure you're okay, that's all."

"He has a father complex," Pearl said.

Norma swallowed. She left the doorway, crossed behind the desk and stopped by the chair. She took his head in her hands and kissed his forehead.

"Hey! What the ..."

Without a word, she turned and crossed the floor, passed through the door with Pearl's deep chuckle following her, and closed the door after her. She ran a finger over her eye to wipe away the single tear, and descended the steps. She crossed the midway, stooped under the rope, went to the rear of the dressing tent and entered.

The four girls were getting prepared for the performance. They turned when she came in. They all started at once.

"Didja see the papers?"

"Geezus what a thing!"

"Imagine him being here the same night he gets knocked off."

"A big gangster!"

"What did you think? Did ya read about it?"

"I saw the paper," Norma said. This was going to be difficult, but she steeled herself to make the effort. She had to be calm. Don't say too much. Just answer the questions. Don't be too interested.

"Where you been?" Darla exclaimed. "I come in this morning and you were gone and I didn't see you all day."

"I was ..." Norma paused. Hanging on a hook by her dressing table was the white terry-cloth robe which Speed had given her. "How did this get here?" she asked.

"Speed brought it in," Darla said. "He said you might want it."

Norma went to the robe and touched it with both hands. If only it can be, she said to herself.

"Where were you?" Darla asked. "Soon as I saw the paper I came looking for you."

"I was with Speed," Norma said, turning.

A comb clattered to the table and Norma looked at Lolly who was staring at her, a mixture of hurt and anger in her eyes. Norma remembered the excitement Lolly had shown about her date with Speed.

"Oh," Darla said, nonplussed. "Oh, well, I didn't wanta be nosey."

Lolly picked up her comb slowly and ran it through her hair. Her face in the mirror was stern. "That's funny," she said in a slow clipped tone, "I was with Speed until four this morning."

Norma did not answer. She busied herself with undressing and applying the oil to her body.

Lolly picked up a copy of the newspaper. "I wonder who this mystery woman is?" she asked.

"The woman in white," Peggy said. "Sounds exciting."

"Don't you have a white dress, Norma?" Lolly asked.

"Yes," Norma said. "It's something like the one you were wearing last night."

"Yes," Lolly mused, staring into her mirror. "But I was with Speed." She let the statement hang in the air and the other girls looked at one another.

"I guess that ends my job," Norma said, eager to get the conversation on a different tack.

"Yeah, ain't that too bad. But imagine, working in a joint owned by the mob," Darla said. "I've heard about that bunch. You'd be peddling it in no time, and you'd never see any of the loot."

"You're probably lucky," Peggy said.

"Luckier than Frank Marco," Lolly said with heavy insinuation.

Norma had difficulty controlling her hands. She knows, she thought. At least she's putting things together. Why did I have to mention Speed? I didn't think about Lolly. She's jealous now. She wants Speed. She keeps looking at that robe.

Norma leaned close to the mirror, making up her face. She was tense and the small mascara brush was shaky. She bit down on her lip. From the corner of her eye she could see Lolly looking at her. Lolly had a small smile on her face, a knowing smile that went deep beyond her eyes.

She knows! She knows! Norma felt the panic rising within her. She resisted the impulse to get up and leave the tent, and run. Run and keep running! No, you can't do that. She doesn't know, she couldn't. She's guessing, but she could never prove anything. But she could go to the police. Speed had said that a carny would never do that. Did that include a woman who was jealous?! Why doesn't she say something? Oh, God, this is going to drive me crazy! Speed, Speed, help me!

Darla and Peggy returned. They clattered down the steps, whipping the capes off their shoulders. "I don't know why they still bother with the bally," Darla said. "That crowd is fighting to get in."

"It's because our star gets so much publicity," Lolly said, the smile still on her lips.

Norma kept her eyes averted and touched the rouge to the tips of her breasts. She could hear the people entering the tent, then the music began and Wendall's voice was on the inside speaker.

Lolly got to her feet and climbed the stairs. She stood poised by the opening in the canvas, then she slipped through.

"Wow!" Darla said. "You rubbed that kitten the wrong way. She's had the hots for Speed since we started the season. Last night was the first time he gave her a tumble."

Norma said nothing. She got up, brought the robe off the hook and draped it over her shoulders. She went to the folding chair and sat down.

"I can't get over it," Darla said. "That good-looking stud with his head bashed in."

"Them gangsters always get it," Peggy said.

Their voices droned on, mingled with the beat of the combo, the shouts of the audience, the whistles, and the steady muted sound of the crowd in the midway. Norma was deep in her own thoughts. If only this had been a one-nighter, she thought. Nothing would have happened. We would have torn down and we'd be miles away by now. But it wasn't. You can't talk away what has happened. It is with you and will stay with you. Would she ever get over it? Would she ever be able to forget the look on Marco's face? She closed her eyes and held her fingers tightly to her temples. Her head was beginning to ache.

Lolly finished her act and came off. She still smiled contentedly and the smile began to grate on Norma's nerves. If only she knew what was going on in Lolly's mind.

"Here I go," Darla said. "The boys in the front row better stand back." She slipped through the canvas.

"They got extra cops out there tonight," Lolly said. "They looked me over like I was a freak."

Norma started, catching her breath. The sound was audible and when her eyes flew to Lolly, the girl's smile had broadened.

The girls went on one after the other, then Norma standing on the small platform listening to Wendall's flattering introduction and waiting for the initial beat of the drum.

Lee! She had practically forgotten he existed. In a moment his eyes would be on her. Was it only last night that she felt so much hate for him? Time, time! How could it go so quickly. Now she felt nothing for Lee. He seemed so insignificant to her. And it was only last night that he had been with Della.

The beat! She pulled the canvas aside and slipped through. It was dark in the tent. The fire burned in the center of the stage. The flames flickered across the expectant faces at the edge of the stage, threw wavering shadows against the top of the tent. She moved halfway down the ramp and stopped. She posed, her arms out, her legs spread and bent at the knee. She threw her head forward, then jerked it back. She came down the ramp, her body undulating, coiling and recoiling, following the message of the drums. Her body glistened in the flickering light as she whirled past the flames, the high, large breasts trembling in the mock offering of sensuality.

CHAPTER FIFTEEN

Norma hurried along the midway. She wanted to go to Speed, but she had the feeling that Lolly would be watching and she was afraid. She stooped under the rope and started across the field to Darla's trailer. The rain increased and she broke into a run.

She was breathless when she reached the trailer. The light was on and she was glad that Darla was there. It would give her someone to talk to and she didn't want to be alone with her thoughts. She wrenched the door open and leaped inside, slamming the door after her.

Lee was sitting on the small divan. Norma looked to the left, but Darla was not there.

"What are you doing here?" she snapped.

"I'm usually here, ain't I?" He was half-smiling.

"Get out!"

"Now wait a minute, baby, don't get into an uproar. I wanta talk to you.

Norma jerked the door handle and flung the door open. "I said, get out!"

"Look, baby, last night was just one of those things. I can explain..."

"I don't want to listen. Just clear out!"

The smile left his face. He lurched to his feet. He grabbed her arms and pushed her back against the wall panel. He gripped her hair, pulling her head back, and he forced his mouth down upon hers. His hands ran over her. He lifted his head and looked down at her. She did not resist, but her expression was cold.

"Are you finished?" she asked.

He still held her. A smile tilted his mouth. "You'll warm up, baby. This is old Lee." He ran his free hand lightly over her breast. Heaving away from the wall, she pushed him back. He stumbled and sat on the divan.

"I don't want you to touch me," she said through clenched teeth. "I saw a hundred just like you tonight. I don't need you, and I don't need them. If you won't get out, I will." She turned and jumped through the open door. Her feet touched the ground and she ran towards the midway. The tempo of the rain had increased. It spattered against her face, light and cooling. The wind had increased and it whispered through the surrounding trees.

"Norma, wait!"

She heard his feet hit the ground and she plunged into the darkness. Her skirt whipped about her legs and billowed out behind her. The rain streamed down her face. He was close behind her and she ran wildly.

He brought her down with a tackle and she screamed as she hit the wet grass. She turned on him before her momentum had ceased. She kicked, screaming, and raked him with her nails. He grunted, his breathing was hard, and he fought back, grappling to secure her wrists. He held her with his legs and found her hands. He pressed her down. She brought her head forward, her teeth bared. He released her hand and slammed the back of his hand across her face. Her head jerked back and hit the ground.

"Listen to me!"

"No! No!" She flailed at his face with her free hand. He hit her again.

"Listen!"

"Speed!" Her voice rose to a high wail. "Speeeeeeeeeeed!"

"Shut up, damn you!" His palm cracked against her wet face. She kicked her legs and fought with renewed fury.

"Speeeeeeeed! Help! Speed!" Her cries were mingled with sobs and anguished groans.

They were in the midst of the trailers and lights began to go on around them. Doors slammed open.

"What's wrong?" a male voice called.

Lee clamped his hand over her mouth. She bit down until she tasted blood. He jerked his hand away.

"Bitch!"

"Help!" she screamed. "Oh, please, help! Speed! Speed! Help!"

Flashlights played through the teeming rain. Footsteps pounded. Lee jumped to his feet. He looked about wildly, but the lights were converging on them. Norma huddled on the ground and cried.

"What's going on here?" It was Gus' voice and he played his flash on Lee's face. "Oh, it's you, Harker."

Della was behind him, a wrapper held tightly about her. "What's wrong?"

The flashlights and the dark forms behind them formed a half-circle. The lights swept down on Norma.

"You bastard, Harker." Gus snarled. "If you hurt this kid." He dropped to his knees and his hands went under Norma's shoulders. Her body shook and she cried hysterically. "Get me away from him"

The circle grumbled with a sullen anger.

"I didn't do anything," Lee said. "She's outta her head." He swiveled his head at the group of unseen forms and his voice quavered with fright.

"Speed," Norma whimpered. "Speed.'

"I'm here." His voice was flat. He stood over her, but he was not looking at her. He faced Lee Harker and he advanced slowly. Lee backed away.

"Now wait a minute, Lamston." He held his hands out, palms up. The rain poured down, plastering his black hair over his forehead. He backed into the circle of lights and stopped. Hands pushed him back. His voice broke. "I didn't mean it. Don't. Listen a minute. Lamston, wait."

Speed's arm shot out and the fist drove hard into Lee's midsection. The drummer gasped and clutched his stomach. He dropped to his knees.

"Get up."

"No, no, please." He covered his face with his hands and began to weep. "Don't hit me," he blubbered. "Don't hit me."

Turning away, Speed bent down over Norma. He swept her up in his arms and walked away from the ring of lights.

One-by-one the lights receded until there was only the darkness and the pitiful sobbing.

Speed walked slowly. The rain beat against him and his anger gradually subsided.

The door of his trailer was open the way he had left it. He stooped inside and crossed to the bed. He put Norma down. He went to the door and closed it. He came back to the bed and leaned over her. He unbuttoned the wet blouse and pulled it off her arms. He removed her shoes, then the skirt. She caught at his arms as his hands went to the hasp of her bra.

"Have to," he said simply. "Everything is wet."

Her hands dropped away. He unfastened the bra and pulled it away. When he was finished he lifted her again. With one hand he pulled back the blankets. He slid her into the bed and pulled the blankets over her. He left her.

"Speed," she cried.

"I'm just getting a towel," he said. He prowled through the dark and came back to the bed. He looped the towel under her head and began to dry her hair.

She closed her eyes and her body began to relax. She felt the strength of his hands and she listened with contentment to his breathing.

"Speed."

"Um?"

"Lie down next to me."

"I'm all wet."

"I don't care. I want you next to me."

He shifted his bulk on to the small bed and stretched out next to her. She lifted her arms from beneath the blanket and encircled his chest. His breathing was against her face. The blanket was between them, but she could feel his heartbeat.

"Speed," she said softly, "could I learn to ride the drome?"

"Sure. Nothing to it."

"Teach me. I want to learn. I don't want to dance anymore. I don't want them looking at me."

"I'll teach you."

"When?"

"When we leave here. We better just keep things the way they are until we get outta here."

She was silent for a long moment. She savored the musty smell of the wet clothes mingling with the odor of sweat. His breathing was heavy and near sleep.

"Speed?"

"Wha'?"

"Don't ever let anyone touch me again," she whispered. "I couldn't stand it if anyone ever touched me again."

His arms went around her and he drew her close to him. "I won't," he said. He was all man and lover as she wanted him to be always.

CHAPTER SIXTEEN

The rain had ended and a mist rose from the midway under the morning sun. The air was clear and moist. Water still dripped from the trees and the canvas gave off a pungent oily smell as it dried.

Norma scowled over the morning paper. Both the cab driver and the ticket clerk had reported to the police. The bus driver had been interviewed in St. Louis. He did not remember a woman in a white dress, but he also stated that he did not remember any of the other passengers either. The police were continuing their investigation, but the newspaper presumed that the woman had returned to St. Louis. Marco's colleagues offered no help, and his destination was unknown when he left the Paradise Club.

Folding the newspaper, she put it aside. She sighed with relief. Her ruse had worked.

Now, if she could ever get over what happened, there might be a chance for her. Please let it happen, she begged, please let it happen.

She slept and when she awoke it was dark and Darla was gone. She leaped up and threw on the light. She glanced at the clock The first show would be starting, but there was time. She left the trailer and walked quickly across the grass. She reached the dressing tent and ducked inside.

"You just made it," Darla said. "Lolly's already on."

"I was asleep." She went to her place and undressed quickly.

"We're using a phonograph tonight," Darla said. "You'll probably have to dance to the Dark-town Strutter's Ball."

Norma did not give it much thought. She certainly knew the dance well enough to do it without Lee. She oiled her body and bent over her make-up.

Lolly came off and Darla went up the steps. "Well," Lolly said, slipping into her chair, "I hear you made quite a stir last night."

Norma ignored her and concentrated on the make-up. She had almost forgotten Lolly's anger.

"Speed came to the rescue, I hear," Lolly said. "Well, I guess some guys never learn."

Holding her breath, Norma forced herself not to answer. Her head was beginning to ache again.

"You got a special fan club out there tonight," Lolly said. "I wouldn't be surprised if you made the headlines."

Norma's fingers tensed. You're too jumpy, she said to herself. She's just trying to get you. Relax. She's mad, but she'll get over it. And after this week you won't be dancing anymore.

Wendall made his pitch and the record went on. Norma listened. *The Song of India.* The beat was all wrong. She looked back and Lolly was smiling. "I picked it for you," Lolly said. Norma bit her lip. She turned and stepped through the canvas. The blinding spot lights struck her. She stood at the top of the ramp. For a moment she was startled and confused. There was no fire in the center of the stage. She was greeted by whistles. Her hands flew up and covered her breasts. This was Lolly's idea of vengeance. Well, this she could weather. Despite her anger, she felt relief flooding over her. She forced a smile, stepped off in time to the music, and stalked down the ramp.

She circled the stage, shaking her shoulders. She went into a series of slow, undulating grinds. She leaned over the edges of the platform, concealing her breasts, and changing to modest bumps.

Her hands flew to her mouth to stifle a scream and she stopped. She stood rooted to the edge of the stage, then she began to back away.

The night clerk from the hotel stared up at her, his eyes wide. She backed away and her heels touched the ramp. The clerk whirled and pushed his way through the crowd.

A cry left her throat. She spun about and ran up the ramp. The crowd shouted after her. The music pounded on. She tore the canvas aside and stumbled down the steps. She stopped in the middle of the dressing tent. She stared at Lolly, her eyes wide with terror and loathing. Lolly smiled. Norma's hand shot out. It cracked across Lolly's face and the girl screamed.

Snatching her robe, Norma fled from the tent. She jammed her arms into the sleeves and pulled the robe about her, knotting the belt. She ran to the edge of the tent and slipped under the rope.

"Police! Police!" The clerk floundered through the midway crowd running for the entrance. His high whining voice echoed above the crowd noise.

Norma clutched her throat. It was constricted. Breathing was difficult and her pulse raced. She backed away, stumbling into people who stared at her with curiosity. The clerk's voice came to her again. She clutched the robe tightly to her throat.

A motorcycle engine exploded into action on her right. She turned. Speed was starting the machine on his bally platform. She pushed through the crowd. Speed had the machine going on the rollers and a crowd was gathering to watch him. He sat astride the saddle and gunned the engine.

"Speed!" she screamed. He did not hear her. "Speed!" She fought through the press of onlookers. She reached the steps and ran up to the platform. He saw her and looked perplexed. She ran to him.

"He's here!" she screamed.

Speed tapped a finger against his ear and shook his head. The machine wavered on the rollers.

Tears spilled over her cheeks and she clasped her hands before her, imploring him to listen. He cut the gas and the cycle coughed and rolled to a stop. He balanced it with his feet.

"He's here!" Norma screamed, her voice still geared to the noise.

Speed held up a hand and she lowered her voice. "The clerk. The hotel clerk. He was at the show. He saw me. Lolly brought him." The words tumbled off her lips. "He ran out. He's getting the police." Her head swiveled towards the midway entrance.

"Norma, Lolly wouldn't…"

"She did!" Her voice rose hysterically. "Look!" She pointed and Speed's eyes followed.

Two uniformed policemen were pushing through the crowd on either side of the midway. There was a hurried purpose in their movements.

"What'll I do?" Her voice became small and pleading. "Speed, help me."

His eyes went from the girl to the policemen and back. Below him the growing crowd watched the scene with curious eyes, wondering what the girl had to do with the act.

"Okay," Speed said. He swung off the cycle. Hefting the handlebars, he dragged the stripped-down Harley-Davidson off the rollers and wheeled it across the platform. He looked up the midway. The two cops were drawing closer. He motioned to Norma with his head and she came to his side. "When I start it, you get on the seat."

He swung his leg over, retarded the spark. He pulled the starter lever up with his toe. He kicked it down. The motor was primed and still warm. It popped and roared. He twisted the spark and the gas. "Okay," he shouted. Norma climbed on the seat behind him. She put her arms around his waist. He put her hands together. "This is going to be rough," he shouted. "These stunt bikes don't have any springs. So hang on!"

It was hopeless. He knew it. A little man was dragging at one of the cop's arm and pointing. So now they saw them. They might get away from the carnival. But they couldn't get away from the police. Two people on a motorcycle. Impossible. He took a deep breath. It was just a gesture. She needs a gesture, he thought, probably the first one in her life.

He gunned the motor and edged the machine towards the steps. It was equipped with a siren for attracting crowds to the bally platform. He kicked the siren off. It wailed and he went off the top step.

The stunned crowd suddenly realized what was happening. They fell away from in front of the steps. The cycle bounced to the bottom. The siren was screaming and Speed jerked the throttle over as they touched the ground. The cycle dug out. The panic-stricken screams of the crowd matched the siren. Speed skidded it on the grass and blasted for the entrance. The people fell back like tenpins. Norma closed her eyes and pressed her cheek to Speed's back.

They came off the dirt road and on to the macadam highway. Speed wound the machine up tight and it settled down to a steady drone, the wind buffeting them.

The Harley-Davidson was flatted out, but it was a clunk, an old machine for stunting, not out-running patrol cars. It was just a matter of time.

Speed felt the rear go as they hit the gravel and he was ready for it. He let it slide away, twisting the front wheel to go with it until the tires got footing. The cycle wavered and rocked, then straightened out, and went for another fifteen yards on the left side of the road until it hit the front of the oncoming Mack diesel and exploded like a gnat.

Norma opened her eyes. The roaring subsided in her ears. She heard voices.

"Poor bastard. He was like hamburger."

The voices dwindled away and she heard the sound of a strong wind roaring through a tunnel. Speed is dead. I can't move. I wonder what happened. The voices again, faint, then clearer.

"... still alive?"

She stared straight up. Every bone in her body seemed broken. She could not move, but she did not care. The milky way was in the corner of her vision. As she watched, a star — a lonely hurtling meteor — exploded into the atmosphere.

Her lips moved. "Spe…" The blood welled up in her mouth and spilled over her lips. She closed her eyes.